DARKWATER

Jennifer Hale, orphaned and destitute after the Civil War, arrives at Darkwater full of hope, only to be alarmed by her cold reception. More frightening are the screams of Alicia, the dying mistress of the plantation. Jennifer becomes attracted to Walter Dere, her employer, and then Alicia's death frees Walter to propose to her. However, Jennifer develops the symptoms Alicia suffered and remembers Alicia's ravings about witchcraft. Will she suffer a fate worse than death?

V. J. BANIS

DARKWATER

Complete and Unabridged

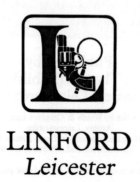

LINFORD
Leicester

First published in Great Britain

First Linford Edition
published 2013

Copyright © 1975, 2012 by Victor J. Banis

*A catalogue record for this book is available
from the British Library.*

ISBN 978–1–4448–1652–5

Second Witch: By the pricking of my thumbs,
Something wicked this way comes.

Macbeth, Act IV, Scene 1

1

Jennifer Hale sheltered in the doorway from the driving rain and watched the approaching cart slip and bounce its way along the muddy track. She felt certain it was coming for her, and at the moment she couldn't say whether she was glad or sorry to see it.

It was only mid-afternoon but as dark as evening. The lights were on in the station behind her and the heat from the iron stove could be felt even here in the doorway. She would have been more comfortable inside but she was too nervous to sit still for long, and the stationmaster's wife had only added to her uneasiness.

'Oh, you've made a mistake,' she said when she learned who Jennifer was and why she had come. 'Alicia Dere will never agree to you.' She said this in a sympathetic tone, but her eyes, bright with excitement, belied the voice.

Now, having spied the approaching cart, she came to stand behind Jennifer. 'That'll be from Darkwater,' she said. 'Why, it looks like the master has come himself.'

Jennifer could see only that the driver of the cart was a big figure swathed in black. It might have been the dark angel himself, come to fetch her, and she shivered a little. She was beginning to regret having come at all. It had been such a long trip, by train from Memphis to Shreveport and from Shreveport here to Durieville, and quite possibly all of it for nothing.

The cart came to a stop at the steps. The man in black jumped down and ran quickly up the steps, his head down against the rain.

The stationmaster's wife, her voice quavering with excitement, was quick to greet him. 'Afternoon, Walter. This here's the young lady you'll be looking for.'

He stepped into the glow of light from the room, shaking some water from his head, and looked down at Jennifer. He appeared startled by her appearance.

Jennifer did not mean to let the moment drag on, giving the plump woman at her elbow more and more to tell her friends later. She thrust a determined hand forward.

'You're Mr. Dere,' she said. 'I'm Jennifer Hale. How do you do?'

His hand came automatically to clasp hers and he mumbled 'How do you do,' in return, but there was no warmth of greeting in either the gesture or the words.

'It was kind of you to come for me yourself,' she said, 'particularly in this weather.' She glanced once toward the stationmaster's wife and then toward the cart. 'My bags are inside.'

His eyes followed hers and to her relief he seemed to understand her concern regarding the stationmaster's wife. 'I'll fetch them,' he said.

She watched him stride to where the porter had left her two bags.

'Sorry to have come in the cart,' he said as he reemerged from the station, 'but it couldn't be helped. We broke an axle on the carriage and I was working on it, but I couldn't get it fixed in time.'

'I don't mind a little rain,' she said. She did not wait but followed at his heels as he took the bags down to the cart. By the time he had loaded them she had already climbed into the passenger's seat without waiting to be handed in. She did not want to give him time to consider things too carefully.

He paused for a moment, looking up at her, before he climbed into the driver's seat and they were off almost at once, the two horses finding their way with little or no direction from him. Jennifer turned over her shoulder to wave goodbye to the stationmaster's wife, who looked a bit disappointed.

Jennifer's sense of triumph, however, was not great. For all she knew she would be back again in an hour or so to face the woman's questioning eyes again. There was no telling how long or how brief her visit to Darkwater might be.

As it was, they did not even get to the house. When they were out of sight of the station, the man beside her guided the horses to the side of the road. He reined them in under the sheltering branches of

6

a spreading oak tree and turned to face her.

'This won't do,' he said without preamble. 'There's no point in even taking you up to the house.'

'I can't see why.' She turned in the seat to face him directly. Rainwater trickled down his forehead in tiny rivulets.

'I think you do. We very specifically asked for an older woman. I told the agency we'd accept nobody under the age of forty,'

'I persuaded the woman at the agency to make no mention of my age when she wrote to you. And if you'll give me any opportunity, I shall try to persuade you to let me have the job notwithstanding my age. I'm quite well qualified, really. I've had experience as a companion, and as a nurse to my ... to someone quite convalescent. I believe that I can convince you of my qualifications.'

Behind his stern countenance she thought she saw the beginnings of a smile. 'Then I'd be better off to take you back to the station now and not give you an opportunity.'

'There are no return trains tonight. And I've already come a very long distance. I had only just arrived in Shreveport before I caught the train for Durieville, after traveling from Memphis, so you can surely see that at this particular moment I am very weary.' She paused and added, 'And very wet.'

He sat for a moment longer, regarding her with no discernible expression. Then he turned forward again and gave the horses a snap of the reins.

'Hospitality is a tradition at Darkwater.' He spoke without looking at her. 'You may stay tonight. Tomorrow I'll bring you in to catch the train back to Shreveport. And I will reimburse you for the trip.'

'I have no desire for charity,' she said a bit sharply, because her disappointment was stinging just behind the lids of her eyes.

'Never mind, I will charge it to the agency that sent you. They should pay, for wasting my time, and yours.'

They rode on in silence. There were a great many things she would have liked to say, but she bit her tongue. It was plain he was already angry and she had no desire to make him more so.

Whatever she might have said out of pride, the truth was, she was very nearly reduced to charity. It would humiliate her to say so but she had not even the money for the return ticket to Shreveport. Coming here had been a desperate gamble. It had taken more than she had anticipated for the ticket, almost the last of her meager funds. She had hoped that in persuading the Deres to overlook her youth she might have a little luck. Now it looked as if it would need a miracle for her to get this job.

She stole a glance at him. He was a very tall man and bundled in his heavy cloak he looked immense. She could see that he had strong hands that were scrubbed clean. Not aristocratic hands, but the hands of a man who worked with them. He was handsome, his face finely chiseled and turned leathery by the sun and wind, so that his pale blue eyes were a shocking contrast. His hair was probably brown by inclination but the sun had streaked it with yellow and even white.

He turned and found her looking at him. For a moment their eyes met. Normally she would have lowered hers as propriety demanded, but she was disappointed and a little angry. She met his gaze boldly. He looked away first.

Maybe, she thought, maybe it wasn't hopeless yet. She pulled her cloak about her and watched what she could see of the passing countryside.

What she could see was water. It not only fell from the heavens but lay on all sides as well. The road ran through the bayou, and all about them stretched the swamp, the surface of the water glistening darkly. Not far away to the left, the land rose. She made out the dim outlines of trees and supposed that Darkwater sat on this higher land.

They soon enough turned to the left. The road began to climb slightly, mounted a rise, and in place of reedy marshes they now passed neatly fenced fields. There were more trees here, and varied vegetation. For a time she had wondered if Darkwater sat in the very swamp, but now she saw this was not so.

After a while they turned again, between two massive gateposts, and went up a drive lined with magnolias dripping moss. Even in the gray light and the rain it looked romantic and lovely. She was grateful they were nearly there. Although it was a warm night, she was soaked through with the rain and she felt chilled, and bone weary.

The house came into view, a splendid, rambling old structure, but less formal and elegant looking than one might expect. She had pictured one of the grand antebellum mansions still scattered about the South, many of them in ruins since the war.

Darkwater was certainly big, but it had more the look of an overgrown farmhouse. The central building was nothing more than a large box, with galleries added to soften the lines a little. From either side, wings extended a considerable distance. It was no architectural marvel, but it looked comfortable to live in.

He left the cart in the drive and hurried

her in through the front door, into a long, narrow hall with wood floors. The lamps here had not yet been lit and the corridor was dark, but from adjoining rooms lamplight cast flickering shadows on the polished wood.

She slipped out of her wet cloak. She was drenched and her bonnet had not prevented her hair from getting thoroughly wet. The bottom of her skirt was crumpled and muddy. She would have liked to look her best just now, if only because it would have given her confidence. Instead, she knew without benefit of the gilt mirror on the wall that she looked like nothing so much as a drowned animal.

He took her cloak, apologizing again for having to get her in an open wagon. He was polite and, in an informal way, quite gracious. There was no sign of the disagreement that lay between them.

A woman emerged from one of the lighted rooms. 'Oh, the lamps haven't been lit out here,' she said, and then, in the same breath, 'There you are, I thought I heard you.'

She came down the hall toward them, a slip of a woman with gray hair and a firm walk. 'I'm Helen Dere, Walter's mother, and you are . . . '

She suddenly paused, close enough now to really see Jennifer despite the dim light. Obviously she was taken aback. She had been about to offer her hand, but it was frozen in midair.

'I'm Jennifer Hale, how do you do,' Jennifer said, clasping the hand firmly in her own.

'There's been a bit of confusion,' Walter said. 'But Miss Hale will be staying the night with us. Have Bess set an extra place for supper and make up the guest bed.'

'Yes, of course.' Helen Dere quickly recovered her poise. 'Alicia's been wanting you.'

'Is she still in bed? The doc said she ought to get up during the afternoons.'

'She says she won't get up unless you come to help her dress.' She glanced sideways at Jennifer, a little embarrassed at this family exchange before a stranger.

'I've got to put up the cart,' Walter said.

'I'll be back in a minute. If you'll see that Miss Hale is made comfortable?'

'Of course.' Helen took Jennifer's arm in a friendly manner. 'You poor child. You look all wet and bedraggled, and you must be dead tired. Why don't I show you to your room and you can have some time to rest and freshen up before meeting the family? Walter, bring her bags up right away, will you? I'm sure Miss Hale will want to change into something dry.'

He went out and Jennifer went along with her hostess, her flagging self-confidence restored a little by the woman's inherent graciousness. She had half-expected a family of pompous wealth and artificial manners, but evidently the Deres were not like that at all. Mrs. Dere's warmth and friendliness was too obviously genuine and Walter himself, despite his stubbornness on the subject of her employment, had been kind and courteous.

Perhaps if she spoke with them frankly and admitted her situation to them, she could persuade them to change their minds and let her stay. At least, with a full evening before her, she had considerable opportunity to plead her case.

Now that she was here, inside the house, she wanted more than ever to stay. It was a lovely home and not only because it was big and well-furnished. It had a welcoming atmosphere. The sitting room that they went past was bright and cozy, with a fire blazing on the hearth, and a big old hound dog before it, who lifted his head to take note of her passing.

'You have a lovely home,' Jennifer said aloud as they started up the stairs.

'Thank you. We've tried to make it that, a home, and not a showplace. Ours is a family that likes to live and not just pose at it, and I like to think Darkwater reflects that.'

The aroma of bread baking drifted from somewhere deep in the house. It mingled with other smells — other foods cooking, the scent of burning pine, of polish and wax and soap. A homely blend of smells and aromas. It was a well-kept home.

Until now the silence had been punctuated rather than broken by the

15

ticking of a grandfather clock, by the creak of stairs beneath their feet, and the sound of the wind and rain from outside. Suddenly it was shattered. Childish laughter floated along the hall, as if on a vapor.

'Such a happy sound,' Jennifer said. 'I believe you can tell a great deal about a house by listening to its sounds.'

Those unfortunate words were scarcely out of her mouth when another, less happy sound pierced the stillness. A woman screamed, and screamed again, a high, wailing shriek.

'Damn her,' Helen Dere said. Then, apparently realizing the impropriety of such a remark in the presence of a stranger, she quickly murmured, 'I beg your pardon.'

'What is it?' Jennifer asked, startled into immobility. 'Who . . . ?'

'Please, it's all right,' Mrs. Dere said, tightening her lips. 'Come, I'll take you to your room.' She put a hand on Jennifer's arm, in a seemingly casual manner, but her grip was firm, brooking no argument.

Puzzled by the outbreak and a little

frightened, too, Jennifer allowed herself to be hurried along the hallway, casting uneasy glances to right and left at the closed doors they passed.

Helen opened one of the doors and said, 'You can have this room for tonight. I'll have someone light a fire for you and bring you some hot water.'

'Please, don't go to any trouble,' Jennifer said, her meager confidence undone.

'It's no trouble. But if you'll excuse me now . . .'

'Yes, please,' Jennifer nodded and then the other woman was gone, leaving her alone in the room.

What a strange place, Jennifer thought. Who could it have been who screamed, and why? Apparently it was not an unusual occurrence, as Mrs. Dere seemed to recover her poise at once, although she was certainly annoyed. She was not alarmed enough, however, to drop everything and go running to see who was screaming and what about. That meant surely that she knew the answers to both questions already.

Jennifer looked around the room. It was cozy, snuggled under the eaves, with a dormer window and an inviting window seat. It was neither opulent nor plain, but a comfortable little room in which it was easy to feel at home.

That was it, she thought suddenly — the feeling of being at home. As if she belonged here, in this house, in this room.

'I think I do,' she said softly, a smile brightening her face.

For some time now she had felt detached from everything. Since her mother's death — no, before that, since the war.

At one time she had felt very much a part of the world, very much alive as only a young woman, healthy, happy, in love, can feel alive. Then had come the War Between the States, and her father had gone to serve. Her fiancé had gone, too.

Neither man had come back, ever, and she'd had to face the war alone, alone with her invalid mother after the servants had gone.

At first her mother had been able to get around and it had not been so difficult.

But then had come the news that her father was dead in battle, and it was as if a mortal blow had been struck her mother too. True, she lived on, through the war and for years afterward until just a few months ago, but she had never recovered from that blow. It was Jennifer who had to carry the ever-increasing burden.

The war. Soldiers. Pillage and looting, and worse. Homes destroyed, and those that were not destroyed, confiscated after the war. The Hales had been reduced from relative prosperity to penury, and in the end, they lost everything.

By then it had not mattered much to Mrs. Hale, who was hardly aware that she lived now in a cheap rented room instead of in her once lovely home. Jennifer had gone to work as a teacher.

At last, perhaps too much later, her mother had died and Jennifer had been left with nothing but a few dollars that she was able to get for their few remaining treasures — and the bills far outweighed those.

Which was how she had come to

gamble on this job in a distant location, and why she felt so strongly the need to secure the job and remain here. It was not only that feeling of belonging here, of being at home.

She had nowhere else to go.

She sighed, and began to remove her muddy dress. She found herself picturing Walter Dere. What an attractive man he was. Thinking of him brought back memories of her dear Johnny. She had thought those memories long banished from her mind, and was surprised, not only to discover them still there, but by their intensity.

She shoved those memories determinedly aside. The dead were gone, all of the past vanished. Those memories must be gone too. She could not afford that sort of romantic dream.

Her dreams now were of nothing more thrilling than survival. And for that, she would need all of her wits about her. She couldn't waste her time or her energy on ghosts from the past.

★ ★ ★

Helen Dere had been oddly impressed with their visitor. It was not only that the young woman was very pretty — you were taken at once with that, of course — or that she was obviously well bred despite the shabbiness of her clothes. Since the war, one had gotten used to seeing people dressed in shabby finery, even here in remote Durieville.

What Jennifer Hale had was a look of strength — soft and subtle, but enduring strength.

Of course she would never do. Alicia would never permit it.

Alicia. That woman! How she had disrupted the peace of an otherwise happy house, with her sickness. *We would be better off if she died,* Helen thought, and was at once shocked at herself.

She hurried back down to the first floor and along that hall, to the rear of the house. A young girl of about fourteen slipped from the door of the room at the end of the hall. The slim figure stood poised for a moment, as if for flight. Then she looked down the hall and saw Helen hurrying toward her, Helen's voile skirt making little swishing sounds as she moved.

The stiffness seemed to go from the girl's body. The shoulders slumped, the head drooped. Her young face took on a lethargic expression and her hands toyed listlessly with the pleats of her skirt, which was patently too short for her.

'What are you doing here?' Helen demanded.

'I came to see Alicia,' the girl said, avoiding Helen's direct gaze. The defensive note in her voice grated badly on Helen's nerves.

'And haven't you been told time and again not to bother Alicia, especially when she's having one of her spells. What did you want with her anyway? What did you do to make her . . . ?'

From behind Helen, Walter's deep voice asked, 'What seems to be the problem here?'

'Walter,' the girl cried. His appearance effected a marvelous change in the girl. Her dispirited pose was abandoned and she was suddenly filled with the vivacity to be expected of a girl her age. She darted around Helen to fling herself wildly into Walter's arms.

'You're back,' she squealed, sounding altogether like a child. 'I missed you so.'

'Now, Liza,' he said, ruffling her hair playfully, 'I was only gone a short while. What seems to be the problem with Alicia? Were you in there?'

Walter could not see the girl's face, buried as it was against his midsection, but Helen saw the quick, calculating look that flashed over it.

'I only wanted to visit with her. I told her I wanted to be friends.'

'That's my girl.' Walter patted her shoulder.

Helen, not in the least taken in, said sharply, 'Why was she screaming? Is that what she thought of your offer of friendship?'

'No, she was screaming because she heard that Walter came back from town with a very pretty lady friend,' Liza said.

Walter's grin faded and he frowned at his mother.

And I'll bet I know who told Alicia about that, Helen thought angrily. She

23

kept that thought to herself and said aloud, 'Liza, I think you had better join the other children and stay out of sight for a while.'

Liza's shoulders automatically stiffened in a gesture of resistance. Walter felt it too and again he patted her shoulder. 'That's right, little darling. It won't do for Alicia to see you if she's in one of those moods, as we all know from experience. You go along now.'

'All right, if that is what you want me to do, Walter,' Liza said, emphasizing the 'you' and casting a quick glance in Helen's directions. She left them, walking sedately for a few feet, like a young lady, and then breaking into a run.

For a moment Helen watched her go with a peevish expression. She loved children and she was well acquainted with their mischief and their ability to dissimulate, but this girl rankled in some way Helen could not quite put into words.

'What makes you frown like that?' Walter asked.

That Walter was completely attached to

the child, she already knew. And she knew too that to express the opinion she had just thought would do nothing more than provoke a quarrel. She ignored his question, and said instead, 'Alicia's been wanting to see you. She's been asking for you ever since you left, even before this latest.'

'It's all right now,' he said. 'I will go to see her.'

He gave her a smile that did not quite erase the signs of fatigue that played around his eyes and the corners of his mouth.

Helen waited until he had disappeared into his wife's bedroom. Then she went along the hall, through the spacious dining room and into the roomy kitchen.

A huge black woman stood before the stove, stirring something in a large pot. In the heat of the kitchen her skin, black as ebony, gleamed as if it had been polished with wax. She was immensely fat, but when she moved, it was with a surprising grace and with the lightness of movement of a nymph, and when she smiled, opening her vast cavern of a mouth to reveal a full array of teeth and pink flesh, she had a unique beauty of her own.

Several blacks worked in the kitchen with her. Two young girls were busy just now peeling potatoes, but this woman, Bess, had an air of assurance that told you plainly she was the queen here, subservient to no one but the Deres themselves, and sometimes she seemed to manage them as well.

She turned from the stove and, catching sight of her mistress's grim expression, said, 'Lord's sake, you look like you've been through the war all over again.'

Although it had been some fifteen years since the war to free the slaves, it remained in Bess's mind as the yardstick by which all other unpleasant experiences were measured. Here at Darkwater it had not made much difference in the lives of the blacks. There had not been so many slaves here as on other plantations and those who were here had lived pretty much the same before the war as after and with nearly as much freedom. The Deres had always been humane people and very progressive in that respect.

Indeed, Bess sometimes pointed out that in some ways things had been better before the war for the blacks here. Prosperity had benefited them as well, and blacks had not always fared well at the hands of Union soldiers either.

She knew, however, that elsewhere blacks had not had it so nice as here at Darkwater. The Deres were the exception, not the rule, and other blacks had plenty of reasons to celebrate their freedom.

These days only a few blacks remained, and they did not do so much farming as in the past. All over the South great plantations had been laid waste, and even many of those that had not been ravaged lay fallow, because the Northerners who had taken them over, breaking them up into little farms, were not farmers, or did not understand cotton or the Southern climate or the intricacies of growing cane.

The Deres had been fortunate in that, even before the war, much of their money was invested in the industrial North, so that their fortune had not suffered so much as their neighbors'. Moreover, Durieville was only a backwater town, not on the road to anywhere, and so had experienced little actual damage from the war.

'It's Walter,' Helen said absentmindedly. 'He looks so strained. All this business of an invalid wife . . . '

Bess gave a disdainful snort. 'Invalid? I'd say puttin' on, if you was to ask me.'

'Now, Bess, I can't believe anyone would voluntarily go through all Alicia's gone through,' Helen argued, but without the strength of conviction to her voice. 'You've seen her when she is having her spells, she really does suffer.'

'The doctor said,' Bess began, but Helen had heard this tirade countless times before.

'Lest I forget,' she interrupted, 'we have a guest. I've put her in the green room and we will need an extra place for dinner.'

'Yes'm,' Bess said. 'This'd be the new nurse for Miss Alicia?'

That there was a guest in the house was hardly news to her. In fact, she had been informed of it when the cart first turned up the drive, as she was promptly informed of nearly everything that went on about the plantation. She had seen the newcomer even before Helen had. Peeking through a crack in the door as they alighted from the cart, her eyes had become wide circles of white in her black face and she had murmured to herself, 'Land's sake, wait until Miss Alicia has a look at her. Umm hummm.'

She looked now entirely innocent, however, as she turned her attention once more to the pot on the stove. The boy had brought her a huge bowl of peeled potatoes, which she snatched from his hand wordlessly, making him look disappointed that he had not been thanked as he was used to.

'Go on,' she said out of the side of her mouth, shooing him away.

'No, our guest will only be staying the night,' Helen said. She did not offer any further explanation. She knew full well that Bess had already seen the newcomer and would figure out for herself why she would not be staying. She left the kitchen.

Bess grinned to herself and added the potatoes to the pot, making brown gravy splash down the sides.

She had been with the Deres since she was born, and was attached to them, especially to Miss Helen, who was her contemporary, with a passionate devotion. During the war, when other slaves, including some who had, as she put, 'been treated like family by the Deres,' were running away or burning and looting their former masters' houses, and the Dere men had been away, Bess had guarded her mistress with an ancient flintlock, defying anyone, white or black, blue or gray coated, to enter the house uninvited. No one had.

Miss Alicia was something else. She was not a Dere except in that she had married Mr. Walter. 'More's the pity,' Bess would say often. It was plain to Bess that there was a war going on right here in this house, between the Deres, especially Walter and his wife, Alicia. That woman was trying to break that man, and she was winning, wearing down his spirit, trying his temper and his patience.

Lord knows, he had been patient enough with her moanings and cryings and screamings. Bess didn't see how he had kept his head for so long, but he was changing. He, who had once been so happy and smiling all the time, and never worried about a thing, not even in the worst of the war, and he hardly smiled at all now, or if he did, it was so tinged with sorrow and tiredness that he looked like a different man.

And where will it all end, she asked herself silently, tasting the stew in her pot? A house divided against itself cannot stand. That was what Mr. Lincoln had said and it was true. She had seen the omens herself, even if Miss Helen ordered her not to practice the arts anymore. Something was going to happen here, something bad, and it was coming soon, she was as sure of it as sure could be.

'It'll be her that brings trouble on the house, too,' Bess told herself grimly. 'With all her mysterious aches and pains and the doctor can't find anything wrong with her except she's spoiled and a Longstreet, and they always thought they was too good for anybody. And she can't stand to think anybody else is happy or having any pleasantness.'

For a fleeting moment Bess's thoughts left that subject and went to the visitor. Well, of course, there was going to be trouble there. Miss Alicia was never going to put up with having someone young and pretty like that around the house.

'Lord knows, and she knows it too, Mr. Walter isn't getting any loving from the woman he's married to,' she said, muttering to herself. 'And a pretty face like that could turn a man's head easy enough.'

The door opened noiselessly and Liza slipped into the room, moving quietly, the way she always did. *Like a rat*, Bess thought.

'And you are another one, always bringing trouble,' Bess said aloud, eyeing her darkly and with no welcome. 'What you been up to in Miss Alicia's room, making her holler? You take her a snake or what?'

'I didn't do anything,' Liza said,

running her fingers along the edge of the table and casting hungry glances around the kitchen for something to eat. 'I went to visit her, and I just happened to tell her about the pretty lady that came in with Walter, and she started hitting the pillow with her fists and screaming.'

Bess chuckled at the picture, for although she considered Liza odd and a nuisance, that feeling paled to nothingness beside her dislike for Alicia.

She quickly recovered herself and assumed a stern expression. 'You go on now, get out of here,' she said, 'and don't be piecing before dinner.'

'I'm hungry. I want something to eat,' Liza said, undaunted by what she called the black woman's 'airs.' 'You can't stop me from getting something to eat.'

Bess's eyes flashed angrily and she shook a long wooden spoon in the girl's direction. 'Go on, git, or I'll tell Mr. Walter.'

The girl's own eyes grew menacing, but she said defiantly, 'He doesn't care about my coming into the kitchen. You can't scare me away.'

Bess leaned toward her until their faces were only inches apart and they stared eye-to-eye at one another. Bess said, in a voice so low it was almost a whisper, 'I'll tell him about the time last week when you put that spider in Miss Alicia's tea and you didn't think I was watching you do it.'

Lisa's face paled and her jaw dropped open a little. For a moment she held her ground but Bess's wide grin undid her and with an angry toss of her head, she whirled about and ran toward the door.

Bess chuckled to herself. In fact, she had not seen Liza do that, but when the spider had showed up in Miss Alicia's tea, she'd had a good idea right away how it had gotten there.

At the door to the outside, Liza turned back and gave a malignant glare. Then she went out, letting the door slam, before Bess had seen her expression.

2

By the time she came down to dinner, Jennifer had restored both her usual neat appearance and her self-confidence. She would somehow convince the Deres to let her stay on here as the nurse-companion that the young Mrs. Dere was said to need. And she had learned over the past few years that desperation often made it possible to do the impossible.

Helen Dere awaited her in the parlor. Although it was summer, a small fire had been lit to fight the damp chill of the storm. The look Helen gave her guest seemed balanced somewhere between instinctive approval and reasoned misgiving.

'My, you look pretty,' she said with sincerity but with a touch of regret, Before, wet with rain and tired from her travel, this young woman had still looked pretty, but now, her hair neatly tied back, her face glowing without benefit of rouge, she looked lovelier still. She wore a gown of pearl gray silk and although it was plainly not new and was well worn, it was a Worth, and still stunning. The absence of jewelry or adornment of any kind only enhanced the effect of old elegance.

'Thank you,' Jennifer replied, glad that she had decided to wear this, the last 'good' dress she had left. Tonight of all nights she must be at her best. 'I'm afraid I must have looked dreadful when you saw me earlier. I'm sure you must have been disappointed at first sight.'

'On the contrary, your appearance was rather more than I expected. Shall we go in to dinner? I should perhaps have explained, we dine rather informally at Darkwater. Since the war, there have been fewer servants and everyone works much more than before.'

'I understand,' Jennifer said. 'We too went through the war. We lost . . . everything.'

With a flash of insight Helen realized that the young woman walking beside her had lost far more than what they here at Darkwater had lost, and it made her more sympathetic to Jennifer's plight. Still, there was always the problem of Alicia . . .

'Of course we were so much more fortunate than most,' Helen said lamely. She knew so many had lost, as Jennifer had said, everything. Families, once proud, aristocratic, wealthy, had been reduced to living in abject poverty, on the tenuous charity of friends. Even a decade and a half after the war the South lay ravaged, and most of the wealth was in the hands of the Northerners who had descended upon the fallen Confederacy like swarms of locusts. Every night when she said her prayers, she thanked God that the Deres, had come through it so well, in large part thanks to her husband's business foresight.

'You have your home,' Jennifer said simply. 'That is fortunate. What a pleasant room.'

The dining room was large and homey, dominated by a long table set informally. The dishes were mismatched and some of them chipped. Another couple was already seated at the table, with them three children: a boy about five, a girl who was obviously his sister and appeared to be about eight, and another girl who was older, probably fourteen, Jennifer guessed, but who looked not at all like the other two.

The adults stood as the two women came into the room, and Helen introduced them. 'This is our guest, Miss Jennifer Hale, This is Susan Donally, my daughter, and her husband, Martin. They live in the cottage just behind Darkwater but they usually take their meals with us. We are somewhat isolated here, so we take comfort in one another's company.'

'You're fortunate it's so quiet tonight,' Susan said. She had a big, open smile and she made no effort to conceal her curiosity regarding their visitor. She was perhaps twenty, and Jennifer recognized her as typical of the generation that had grown up since the war, without the old forms of courtesy and rigid formality. 'Anyone who happens to be passing by about this time stops in for dinner — people from town, neighbors, relatives, even traveling salesmen.'

'Hospitality is a tradition here,' Helen said.

'We're friendly folk, that's for certain,' Martin Donally said. 'Comes from being stuck out here in the back country.'

'That fact also saved us from the fate that befell most of the South,' Helen said.

Like his wife, Martin was friendly and blatantly curious. They seemed to Jennifer surprisingly inelegant for this family. Despite a certain roughness, Walter Dere had the unmistakable stamp of class and his mother was obviously aristocratic, but Martin and Susan were like simple country people — cheerful, rough and unpolished.

'And the children?' Jennifer asked, indicating the three at the table who had been staring openly at her. 'Surely they can't be yours.'

Susan gave an embarrassed little laugh and said, 'Heavens, no, those are Walter's children.'

'That is to say,' Helen corrected her quickly, 'the two young ones are Walter's. This is Peter, and Mary. And this is Liza.'

Jennifer noted that no one tried to

39

explain whose child Liza was. She wondered if she should ask and decided not. The omission had been deliberate. An awkward little pause followed, which might have became embarrassing had not Walter himself come into the dining room just then.

He had not taken time to change his clothes. His suit still hung damply about him and he had the look of a harried man. Despite this, though, Jennifer could not help remarking to herself what an attractive man he was.

At first glance, one might not necessarily think Walter Dere so attractive. He was ruggedly built, and his big powerful body lacked the sort of slim elegance that one expected in a Southern gentleman, but when he moved, he moved with surprising grace, quick and catlike, and with no wasted motion. His face was not conventionally handsome, either, the features were too florid. He had piercing eyes and thick dark hair, which spilled over his forehead in wayward fashion. His nose was rather prominent, his lips thick, and his chin square.

He had an extraordinary magnetism, however, and an aura of strength that appealed at once to a woman. When he smiled, his mouth lost some of its cruel sensuality and his eyes softened. His voice was low and gentle; he was completely manly, without being crude, polished without being effeminate. The sort of man other men liked and to whom women were attracted, and it was perhaps his most endearing quality that he remained quite unaware of the impression he made on others.

Now, he paused inside the dining room and said, without preamble, 'Alicia is joining us.'

A little shock wave of surprise rippled about the table. Helen was the first to recover. 'Come along then, children,' she said, 'You will eat in the kitchen. Hurry, now.'

Without argument, as if they were glad to go, the three children jumped up, helping her to clear their places, and in a moment they were gone into the kitchen. Susan sprang into action, rearranging the places that remained, so that in hardly

41

more than the blinking of an eye, it was as if the children had never been there and the table had always been set for six adults.

Alicia is their mother, Jennifer thought, amazed that it should be necessary to spirit the children away. They were, after all, quiet and well-mannered and should not have been expected to disturb their mother, even if she were ill. Or was it merely the sight of them that disturbed her, so that they had to be removed from sight whenever she came around?

Helen came back from the kitchen, where she had set the children at a wooden table there. And not a moment too soon, Jennifer reflected, for a moment later there was a sound in the hall and a gentle cough as someone approached the dining room.

Walter went into the hall and Jennifer heard him say, 'Why didn't you call me? I'd have come and helped you.'

'And have everyone laugh about how helpless I am?' A woman's voice, high and reedy, said. 'No, thank you, I'm not quite dead yet. More's your regret, I suppose.'

'Alicia,' Walter said in a tone of gentle reproach.

They came into the dining room and it seemed to Jennifer that not only conversation but the passage of time itself was momentarily suspended. She saw the woman's eyes, dark and glittering like those of a hawk, sweep the room until they found and fastened on her.

Alicia Dere had been pretty at one time, and she had still a trace of hard beauty about her, but she was thin now to the point of gauntness and her features stood out sharp and harsh, so that she seemed to be without curves and all angles. Black shadows under her eyes suggested insomnia to Jennifer. She looked nearly as old as Walter's mother.

'Well, hello,' Alicia greeted Jennifer with a bright smile that was so artificial it was ghastly. 'And you are Walter's friend, the young woman he brought back from town with him.'

'I am Jennifer Hale,' Jennifer replied, careful not to show that she had found the description offensive. 'I came about the job.'

'About the job?' Alicia feigned surprise. 'But that is quite ridiculous. They were sending an older woman. That's what they promised us. I insisted on an older woman.'

Before Jennifer could speak, Walter said, 'The agency made a mistake, but it was too late for Miss Hale to return tonight. She is spending the evening and will be leaving in the morning. We could hardly allow her to spend the night in the station.'

'No, of course not,' Alicia murmured.

Jennifer felt disappointment rising like gall in her throat. She swallowed hard. It would be all the more difficult to press her case after so definite a statement on Mr. Dere's part, and particularly in view of Mrs. Dere's obvious resentment of her. She must think of something to do or say — but what?

'Shall we sit down?' Helen said, stepping into the breach.

They took their places about the table. Jennifer noted that Helen, and not Walter, sat at the head of the table. Walter sat beside his wife, even pulling his chair closer to hers. As the meal began, with the food brought in by a vast colored woman who eyed Jennifer with blunt curiosity, Walter began to spoon feed his wife as if she were a baby. To Jennifer's further amazement, the others apparently took this for granted.

'Come on, now, try a little of this,' Walter coaxed, holding a spoon to Alicia's lips. She made him wait for a few seconds before she parted her lips and reluctantly accepted a morsel of food.

'Everyone knows that I don't care for yams,' she said, rudely spitting the food back out.

'What would you like, then?' Walter asked patiently.

'I would like some of that gooseberry jelly,' she said, pointing at a green tinted jar in the center of the table. 'And a biscuit.'

Susan Donally made an effort to start conversation. 'You look very young to be out on your own,' she said, looking down the table at Jennifer. 'Don't your parents worry about you?'

Jennifer lowered her eyes and said

softly, 'My parents are dead. My father was killed in the war, fighting for the Confederacy. My mother had been ill for some time and the shock was too great for her. She took to her bed and never really left it.'

'I am sorry,' Susan said, but she looked not at all sorry to have satisfied her curiosity.

Helen said, 'That is where you got your nursing experience, then?'

'Yes, although I was trained to be a teacher, and I worked at that job until the last two years, when my mother's health deteriorated to the point where I had no choice but to be with her constantly.'

'A teacher?' Susan said. 'That's interesting. The children here at Darkwater could certainly use a teacher. Their education has been pretty haphazard.'

Martin, her husband, who had been eating with gusto, said, 'I suppose you taught girl children.'

'Why, yes, I did. I taught at a private school for girls. But why do you say so?'

'Well,' he said, grinning, 'I know what boys are like. A little slip of a thing like you would have a hard time keeping a bunch of rowdy boys in line, I would say.'

Jennifer had no intention of being dragged into an argument with a man of his frame of mind, which was, she was certain, that woman was inadequate for any job outside the home. She wondered what he would think if he knew she was in sympathy with the Reverend Henry Ward Beecher and the American Woman Suffrage Association.

Martin was going on and on about the difficulties of managing boys. Jennifer let her glance move around the table.

Walter's wife puzzled her. This was the invalid, and she'd had experience with invalids who were really sick. Alicia was indeed very thin and her color was terrible, a gray, claylike pallor, but she did not look sick. Certainly she had a voracious appetite, for although she still insisted that Walter spoon feed her, and picked and chose what she wanted, she was managing nonetheless to put away plenty of food.

While Jennifer was studying the so-called invalid, Alicia, as if Jennifer's thoughts had intruded upon her own, suddenly stared directly at her and the incident sent a cold chill up Jennifer's spine. This was a woman capable of extreme malice, Jennifer thought as she lowered her eyes to her plate.

'No,' Martin was concluding some lengthy monologue, 'I think teaching is still a man's field. Excepting, perhaps, teaching in a girl's school. And a woman's place is in the home.'

Jennifer turned her luminous eyes on him and said frankly, 'But that presupposes that only boys cause trouble, and that girls do not, but that is simply not the truth. Boys make a great to-do, but girls can be subtle and it sometimes takes wit to see what they are about.'

Alicia pushed aside the spoon Walter had raised to her lips, and she seemed on the verge of saying something, but Jennifer did not notice her and went on.

'The truth is, force alone is not the answer. A teacher must earn the student's respect, or punishment won't have any effect. But I should add, if corporal punishment is called for, I think myself capable of administering it.'

'Even to a girl?' Alicia asked in that thin, wasted voice of hers.

Jennifer was startled by that question from Alicia, who had not spoken since sitting down except to whine to Walter about her food.

'To a boy or a girl if either needs it,' Jennifer said. 'And I do think girls sometimes need it as well as boys.'

To Jennifer's further surprise, Alicia said, 'I think Susan is right, the children here need a teacher, a woman teacher. Someone like Miss Hale.'

The statement was as much a surprise to the others around the table as it had been to Jennifer. Certainly Alicia was the last person present that Jennifer would have expected to say anything in her favor.

'The men we've hired, all they ever do is whip Peter to look like they are earning their salaries. Why is it I never heard of a girl being whipped?'

Still no one made a comment. The people around the table stared at Alicia as if she had perhaps just blasphemed. Jennifer held her breath, fearful that

49

anything she said might cause Alicia to turn against her as abruptly as she had sided with her.

Alicia's claw-like fingers suddenly gripped her husband's wrist, causing him to spill a spoonful of jelly.

'Say that Miss Hale can stay to teach the children,' Alicia pleaded, looking up at her husband with wide, feverish eyes. 'And to be my companion,' she added in a firmer voice. She suddenly turned her gaze on Jennifer again, but this time it was a friendly look.

'That won't be too much work for you, will it?' she asked. 'Acting as both teacher and companion?'

'I . . . I don't know, of course,' Jennifer said. 'That is, I've no idea how much schooling the children will need, nor of how much attention you require in your . . . condition. But I would think I could manage it easily enough, if I am given the opportunity to try.'

'Do say she can have the opportunity, Walter, darling,' Alicia insisted.

Jennifer let her eyes go to Walter's face. Just then he looked at her too, and she had an odd sensation, as if she were suddenly falling, so that she actually gripped the edge of the table to support herself. She had never felt such a reaction to a man before, not even with Johnny, whom she had certainly loved, and it frightened her and embarrassed her. She felt her face growing warm and wondered what the others would think.

But he is married, something within her cried, and she answered herself angrily, *I know that*.

'If it will make you happy, and if it pleases Miss Hale, of course she can stay,' he said, but there was no pleasure in his voice and Jennifer wondered if his thoughts were like her own.

★ ★ ★

Although it seemed to Jennifer that it was very early when she rose and came downstairs, she was surprised to discover that the family had already breakfasted and were about their chores. The children could be seen playing in the yard. The dining room was empty and in the kitchen Helen was going over the inventory of food supplies with the large black woman who had served dinner the night before.

'I'm afraid we breakfast early,' Helen said. 'We all have to do more of the work now, and that means early rising. The men are already in the fields.'

'I must seem like a frightful laggard,' Jennifer said apologetically.

'You had a long journey yesterday,' Helen replied. Her tone implied that while Jennifer need not apologize for sleeping late this morning, she would be expected to adopt the family's schedule in the future. Jennifer did not mind. Usually she was an early riser herself.

'Is Mrs. Dere still abed?' Jennifer asked. 'I mean, that is, the other Mrs. Dere.'

'We have dispensed with a great deal of formality here,' Helen said with a smile. 'And I think you will find it less confusing if you did likewise. I would suggest you call me Helen. As for Alicia, I expect she will want you to call her by her first name, but you had better wait until she suggests it herself.'

'I will. I wonder if perhaps, as Alicia — Mrs. Dere — is still sleeping, I should begin with the children this morning. What do you think?'

'I think there's no particular hurry. There will be plenty of time to get acquainted with the children today and you can start lessons tomorrow, if you like.'

Jennifer started to ask something else and hesitated, not sure exactly how open she could be with the mother of her new employer. It was Helen, after all, who functioned as the mistress of the house. Despite Helen's old Southern char, Jennifer could not help thinking that the older woman disapproved of Walter's decision to hire her, her youth notwithstanding. Jennifer knew that she had been hired only because of Alicia's mysterious support. She had the impression that Helen would have preferred to see her on her way this morning.

'I'm not sure I should ask this,' Jennifer said slowly, 'but I'm not clear on one point and I wonder if you could help me. Am I to teach all three of the children or only . . . only Mr. Dere's?'

Helen stiffened visibly, as if this subject were taboo. 'Liza is treated as a member of the family,' she said. 'At least insofar as we can treat her. She will have her lessons with the other children.'

'I see. Is there a schoolroom here?'

'No, not a schoolroom exactly, but there is the library. I think that will do nicely. Perhaps you will look it over and see if you don't agree. It's just along the central hallway.'

Jennifer went along the hall as directed and found the library with its book-lined walls. At once she loved the room. Thanks to all those books, here more than anyplace else in the house she had a sense of belonging. She could not see a wall of books without feeling something almost sensuous stir within her. She went quickly to a shelf and studied the titles. She found Plato at once, and Marcus Aurelius, but she could see that there was a good sampling of the moderns, like Mark Twain and Henry James. It was not only an extensive collection but an up-to-date one as well.

Someone had been reading and had left a book open upon a table. Curious, she picked it up. It was a volume of Shakespeare's plays, open to Macbeth. Whoever had been reading that tragedy had read it more than once, judging from the book's well-worn condition.

She was startled when a masculine voice behind her said: 'You are a lover of Shakespeare, then?'

She turned to find Walter Dere at the library door.

'I am sorry,' he said, 'I didn't mean to startle you. I was just coming along the hall and saw you there, with my book.'

'Is it your book?' she said, embarrassed. She quickly returned the book to its place on the table. 'I did not mean to overstep the bounds of propriety.'

'Be assured you did not, and please, make use of any book here. I treasure them, but even more do I treasure sharing them with a fellow book lover.'

She felt a bond established between them. Two people who loved good books and fine literature and who were sur-rounded by Philistines.

'I would not have guessed you for a man who cherished books, and certainly not Shakespeare.'

'Odd, I would have said no one could love books without feeling something special for Shakespeare. Did you teach him in that school you were employed at — the one with all the wily girls?'

'Some. When I could keep their attention on him long enough.'

He remained standing half in half out the door, so that he would be visible to anyone passing in the hall, while she was across the entire room from him. Even so, Jennifer was aware of a certain impropriety in this lengthy interview alone with him. But if he was aware, he gave no sign of it.

'Then you must understand him pretty well,' he said.

'Pretty well, I think.'

'Good. There are some points I've often wondered about. Perhaps we can talk about them sometimes and you can help me clear up my thinking.'

She doubted that his thinking was ever anything but clear. Her little warning voice was telling her that this conversation had gone on long enough now and that she ought to excuse herself before someone saw them and got the wrong impression.

'For instance?' she prompted him.

Certainly he seemed to have no interest in ending their discussion. 'For instance, all that supernatural business. Is it literal, or only subjective? I have heard arguments both ways.'

'Both literal and subjective, I should think. In Macbeth, for instance, Banquo's ghost is certainly subjective. It's only Macbeth's imagination at work. But in some other plays he surely means the ghosts and spirits to be taken literally.'

'What about the witches in Macbeth? They are surely not meant literally, are they?'

She shook her head. 'I think not. Macbeth saw them because he wanted to see them. He wanted to remove Duncan from the throne and so he saw three witches who prophesied his doing just that. It was only his ambition talking.'

'But don't you think that makes the

entire play monstrous, because certainly the good in him is defeated and in your interpretation, evil triumphs?'

Jennifer was thrilled to see that his grasp of Shakespeare was far more than superficial. She so rarely met anyone with whom she could truly discuss such things that she was fairly trembling with excitement.

They had been so absorbed, however, in their literary argument that both had failed to hear anyone approach until Helen suddenly appeared behind Walter in the doorway. She looked from one to the other of them, clearly a bit surprised to find them alone together like this.

'I was just coming to see if you thought the library would be all right for the lessons,' Helen said.

'Yes,' Jennifer said, blushing. 'I think it will do very nicely.'

Why is she blushing, Walter thought. *So she feels it too, then? It isn't only me. But, my God, it can't be. And yet . . . and yet . . . .*

He too seemed finally to realize his position, for he said, with what might have been embarrassment, 'I was on my way down to look in on Alicia.'

He turned to go but paused long enough to incline his head toward Jennifer and say, with a barely suppressed smile, 'It has been most enlightening, Miss Hale, and I hope we will have an opportunity to continue.'

'I have no doubt we will continue our discussion,' she said, and with a barely perceptible flick of her eyes in Helen's direction, she added, 'Perhaps we can form a little discussion group and get several opinions.'

'Perhaps,' he agreed, looking vastly amused at that suggestion. Then he was gone. Jennifer heard his footsteps echoing along the hall. A distant door closed. It seemed to her that the light had grown dim in the room.

Helen said, 'Would you like me to bring the children in now? You'll want a chance to get acquainted with them before you actually start lessons.'

'Yes. I will need to know just what they have been taught before, and then there is the question of their textbooks.

What have you here?'

'There are some textbooks there,' Helen indicated one of the lower shelves. 'Whatever else you think necessary can be ordered. I will bring the children.'

She was back in a few minutes, shepherding the three youngsters. Jennifer saw that Peter and Mary looked a bit apprehensive but nonetheless excited at the prospect of a new routine. The oldest of the three, the girl Liza, looked sullen and resentful. Jennifer guessed that, as she was obviously quite a bit older than the other two, perhaps she resented being treated as a child the same as them.

Whatever the reasons, her instincts told her that whatever problems she might have would center around Liza and not the other two.

Helen left them alone in the library. Jennifer faced the three youngsters and said, 'Now then, so we make no mistakes, let us get reacquainted. I am Miss Hale, and will you each please tell me your name again and how old you are?'

'I'm Peter and I am seven,' the boy said.

'Six,' the little girl said.

Peter's bright smile turned to a frown. 'I am almost seven,' he said with an angry look at his sister.

'Very well,' Jennifer interceded, 'Six and a half will do nicely. And you?'

'I am Mary, and I am eight and a half.'

The oldest of the three sat gazing from the window at the green field outside. She pointedly ignored the others in the room.

'Aren't you going to tell me your name?' Jennifer asked her.

'You have already been told my name.'

'Perhaps I would like to hear it again,' Jennifer said firmly. 'And I would like you to look at me when you are speaking to me, please.'

The girl turned then and looked directly at her. Jennifer was startled by her expression. It was not one of girlish temper, as she might have expected, but a look of mature malevolence. For a moment it disconcerted her.

'I am Liza,' the girl said, almost spitting the words at her.

'And how old are you, Liza?' Jennifer asked, recovering her composure. It would not do, she knew from experience, to let this child start off on the wrong foot. It would undo any future attempts at discipline.

'I don't know.'

'You don't know?' Jennifer asked, astonished. The girl only continued to stare at her, now with a blank expression that told nothing of what she was thinking or feeling. 'What of your parents?'

'I have no parents.'

Unexpectedly, Peter cried, 'Her mother is the swamp witch.'

'That isn't true,' Liza cried, leaping to her feet. Afterward, Jennifer was certain that Liza would have struck Peter had not she also risen to her feet and spoken sharply.

'Liza,' she said. The girl froze where she was and looked at her angrily.

'That wasn't true,' Liza said.

'Whether it was or was not, we shall have discipline while we are at lessons,' Jennifer said sternly.

'I am not afraid of you.'

Jennifer was momentarily taken aback by this display of impertinence. She hesitated briefly, not knowing just how far she was permitted to go in disciplining the children.

'You will do as I say or I shall have to speak to Mr. Dere.'

That threat at least had some magic effect. The taut anger seemed suddenly to leave Liza's body and without further argument she returned sullenly to her seat.

Jennifer studied the three faces before her. She saw that Peter and Mary had been impressed with her show of firmness and she guessed she would have no real difficulty with them.

She felt a burning curiosity, however, to know more about Liza. How could she not know her own age? Jennifer had reckoned it to be about fourteen, certainly no more than a year younger or older, but oughtn't she to know that herself? And what an odd thing for her to say, that she had no parents. And who was the swamp witch, who Peter had said was her mother?

She did not ask any of these questions aloud, though, because she felt they were sure to provoke another outburst. For some reason or another, the question of

Liza's parentage was a sensitive subject. Nor was there anyone else she could ask. Her hints in that direction with Helen had produced a coldness that implied she was prying, and she could hardly presume to question Mr. Dere regarding his household. Nor was Mrs. Dere likely to satisfy her curiosity.

A sudden thought crossed her mind as she thought of Mr. Dere. Peter and Mary were his and Alicia's children, and Liza plainly was not. But could she be Mr. Dere's by some other . . . she hesitated even on the thought . . . by some other relationship? That would explain why she was here, why he gave her the same place as his own children. It would explain too the family silence on the subject, and why the children were kept out of Alicia's way.

But these are not my questions to answer, she thought. She returned her attention to the children, who had been waiting silently.

'I think,' she said, 'I will hear each of you read something, so that I can begin to ascertain the extent of your previous education.'

3

From the very beginning, Jennifer was puzzled about one thing in particular: why would Alicia Dere, who certainly gave the impression of being a suspicious and a possessive woman and whose first attitude toward her had been decidedly unfriendly, suddenly take her part in persuading Walter to give Jennifer the job and let her stay on at Darkwater?

It did not take her long to find the answer.

After a few days, a routine had been established in Jennifer's day and she found that even with the two jobs she had been given she was not overworked. Indeed, she had considerable leisure.

In the mornings she worked with the children on their lessons. They were all three bright and although Liza remained sullen and uncommunicative, she had no difficulty mastering the work Jennifer assigned her.

At first Jennifer wondered why Liza even bothered, since she so obviously resented both Jennifer and the lessons, but Jennifer soon came to understand. Liza worked to master her lessons for the same reason that she did almost everything else — for Walter's approval.

'You'll tell Walter how well I did, won't you?' Liza would say when she had done something particularly well. And whenever Liza's work was not up to her best, Jennifer had only to say, 'Think what Walter would say if he knew you could not learn that,' to provoke a veritable orgy of study until that particular lesson had been utterly mastered.

It was clear that the child idolized the man, although Jennifer remained as ignorant as before of the nature of their relationship. Liza was treated as if she were another of his children, or almost so. She ate with the other children, studied with them, had a bedroom next door to theirs upstairs and had even more privileges than they did, because of her greater age.

Yet there was a subtle difference in

Liza's place in the house that Jennifer could not quite put her finger on. She guessed that the others, Helen and certainly Alicia, resented Liza's presence, and perhaps because of that Walter was inclined to dote on her, often at the expense of his own children. Liza seemed to be an outsider, looking in. And Walter seemed . . . but she couldn't find the words for Walter's attitude toward the girl. He seemed blinded to any shortcomings or failings, and to take her adulation for granted.

'But at least,' Jennifer told herself, 'her devotion to Walter gives me the means to keep her in line.'

After each day's schoolwork was finished, Jennifer had what she had always called luncheon but which the Deres pronounced simply, lunch. Usually she ate in the dining room with Helen. Sometimes Susan came in from the cottage, and the children either ate with them or in the kitchen, depending more than anything else on Helen's frame of mind that day. Less often, the men joined them.

'In the old days they would have been here,' Helen said with a look of regret, 'but now they must do so much of the work themselves. During planting and at harvest we hardly see them at all.'

After lunch, Jennifer spent some time with Alicia, who ordinarily had her lunch on a tray. Although when Jennifer had first come to Darkwater, it had been because Alicia was supposed to need a nurse, Jennifer quickly saw that Alicia needed little more than a companion, and especially a listening post for her complaints. It was Jennifer's opinion that there was nothing physically wrong with Alicia, and that opinion was strengthened daily.

Whenever Walter was around, Alicia was at her most helpless, needing assistance even to sit up in bed, but when Walter was definitely away, and Alicia knew that he could not hear or be told of her difficulties, she managed very well for herself.

Of course she was weak and drawn, Jennifer was willing to admit that, but so would be anyone who spent all her time in bed and got no sun or fresh air. It took only a short time of acting as if one were sick to produce actual sickness.

'What you pretend to be,' Jennifer's mother used to say, 'you soon enough become.'

It was plain to all that Alicia favored her new companion, and while everyone of the household, including Jennifer, puzzled over this, they could not help but be grateful for the peace that resulted from it. For a time Alicia had no more of her 'spells' and tranquility, so long absent from the house, reigned.

But Jennifer was still aware, as some of the others were not, of an undercurrent of tension in the air. She had a feeling of something about to happen, of waiting for a curtain to go up.

Walter too seemed to be waiting. Again and again Jennifer discovered him watching her. She would look up from her work to realize that he was standing nearby, staring directly at her. For a moment he would continue to study her; then, without a word of explanation, he would turn and go. Or, while they were at dinner, she would glance across the table to find that, even while he was spoon-feeding his wife, Walter's eyes were on her.

She could not read the look in his eyes. She was not so naïve that she did not know the look of lust in a man's glance, and this did not seem to be that. Nor was it unfriendly or antagonistic. If anything, she would have said he looked as if he were wondering, and perhaps even a little afraid.

Jennifer soon came to understand Alicia's interest in her, however. When she went to Alicia's room after lunch, Alicia made a habit of asking about the children and their progress with their lessons. She asked about Peter and Mary and even went so far as to suggest that some of the children of their neighbors might profit from Jennifer's attentions as well.

'Perhaps,' Alicia said one day, 'we should think about starting up a regular school for the children hereabouts. There's a school in town, of course, for the poorer children. I meant to say, a school for the plantation youngsters.'

Jennifer soon realized, however, that there was only one child in whose progress Alicia was really interested — Liza. Whenever she asked about Liza, Alicia's eyes glistened wickedly and she sometimes actually licked her lips.

'Isn't she just like what you described that first night you were here?' Alicia demanded eagerly. 'Those sneaking girls who are more of a problem than boys and who need more discipline?'

Jennifer was taken aback by this distortion of her own casual remarks. She suddenly realized that it was for this reason Alicia had taken so quickly to her.

'I don't know that Liza is so sneaky,' Jennifer said. 'She's stubborn and in her own way mischievous. She likes to play tricks on the other children, but the tricks are mostly good-natured and the children really seem to get along very well together when there are no adults around.'

She longed to add, 'considering their relationship,' but she dared not. In fact, she still knew nothing of that relationship beyond what she might conjecture. She had no one to ask, and no one volunteered any information, beyond Peter's comment about a 'swamp witch.'

She was soon quite aware, though, that Alicia hated Liza with a jealous passion that was inexplicable. If Liza had been a grown woman and beautiful, as she did indeed give promise of becoming, it might have been understandable, but not even Alicia, who was capable of senseless hysteria, could believe that Walter and Liza were in any way romantically involved.

Now, thinking that she might elicit some further information from Alicia, who on this occasion was in a particularly chatty mood, Jennifer said, 'I do think that she resents her lessons. A time or two I have thought of discussing her with Mr. Dere.'

'No,' Alicia said, so sharply that Jennifer was alarmed by her suddenly heightened color. 'If you have any problems with Liza, you are to come to me with them. That is an order. Do you understand?'

Jennifer had no choice but to nod in agreement. 'As you wish,' she murmured reluctantly, regretting her pursuit of this line of conversation.

'That child needs discipline, that's all that's wrong with her,' Alicia added, her eyes taking on a strange glazed look. 'And you are to see that she gets it. Go to that cupboard there.'

Jennifer went as bidden to the tall cupboard against the far wall.

'Open it,' Alicia said. 'There, on the shelf, that's right. A riding crop.'

Jennifer brought out the riding crop, an elegant piece of equipage that she guessed must have belonged to Alicia's healthier days.

'Use that on her,' Alicia said. 'That will keep her in line. And I forbid you to mention this to anyone else.'

Jennifer was shocked and sickened by the cruel suggestion, but she knew that to argue with Alicia would provoke more hysterics. Wordlessly she took the riding crop with her and left the room. She had no intention of beating Liza but she was not above letting Alicia believe that she would, if it meant maintaining the uneasy peace in the house.

The others discussed the peace, too, and puzzled over it at the same time they were grateful for it.

'It's a blessing having that girl in the house,' Helen said to her daughter.

'Just now, maybe,' Susan agreed without enthusiasm. 'But that girl, as you call her, is a woman, and a very pretty one, too. Sooner or later Alicia's going to change her mind about wanting her here, and when she does, there will be trouble.'

'But she's been so good for Alicia. She hasn't had one of her spells in two weeks now, since Jennifer came.'

Susan gave a derisive snort. 'Spells my foot. Those spells of Alicia's are nothing but jealous fits, and you know it as well as I do. And one of these days she's going to get jealous of Miss Jennifer. Walter's a normal, healthy man, and in some ways he hasn't had a wife for a long time now. How long do you think it will be before he notices how pretty Miss Jennifer is — if he hasn't already?'

'And because he notices someone is pretty, do you think Walter is immoral enough to . . . to do anything about it?' Helen asked indignantly, because Susan's remarks had only added emphasis to her own worries, fears she had been trying not to face.

'That's not the point,' Susan said. 'He won't have to do anything to set Alicia off. All it will take is for her to see him looking at Jennifer — the way a man looks at a woman when he wants her — and there'll be trouble to pay.'

'What nonsense. Why, you've only got to see the two of them together to realize Alicia's devoted to Jennifer.'

Her own fears continued to nag at Helen, though. Jennifer was more than pretty. She was exquisitely beautiful, with her pale skin like fresh cream and her dark hair that hung in ringlets about her shoulders, and those wide green eyes that seemed sometimes to look right through you.

And Walter . . . God knows, Helen thought, Alicia hasn't been a wife to him in two years or more. How long can a

man stand that without his flesh rebel-
ling?

Susan was right about one thing: if
Alicia ever even suspected that Walter was
so much as attracted to the new
governess, she would stop at nothing for
revenge.

★ ★ ★

When the peace was broken by another of
Alicia's outbursts, however, it was Liza
who was the target of her anger and not
Jennifer.

It came about partly because of
Jennifer's attempts to placate Alicia's
hatred of the young girl. After giving the
riding crop to Jennifer and instructing her
to use it to discipline Liza, Alicia did not
mention it for several days. Jennifer
assumed that she had spoken in anger
and either regretted her instructions, or
had even forgotten them.

Certainly Jennifer had no wish to
remind her, and she avoided mentioning
any difficulty with Liza. In fact, she had
no real problems with the girl aside from

her withdrawn attitude. Liza had no interest in anyone or anything except Walter, and pleasing him.

Nearly a week after Alicia had given her the riding crop, Jennifer came into her bedroom to find Alicia in a worked up state that she sensed was a prelude to a real outburst.

'Well,' Alicia said, 'what about Liza?'

'What about her?' Jennifer repeated, her uneasiness increasing.

'Have you used the crop on her yet?' Alicia leaned forward with a look of utter cruelty on her once pretty face.

'I . . . ' Jennifer hesitated to tell an outright lie. 'I have disciplined Liza as it was necessary,' she concluded lamely. It was close to the truth. She had had to rebuke Liza on two occasions for inattention, although she had resorted to nothing more than a mild scolding.

'So,' Alicia said, breathing heavily as if the mere thought of Liza's punishment excited her. 'So she is not the goody-goody after all, but does need some punishment. I've tried and tried to convince the others, but they have always insisted she was a good girl.'

Alarmed that Alicia's mood seemed to be getting out of hand, Jennifer said, 'I don't think I would say she was a bad girl.'

Alicia gave her a venomous look. 'Bad? She's a witch, like her mother. You've only got to look at her to see how evil she is. What do you think is making me so sick? The doctor can't find anything wrong with me physically, he told me that himself. It's witchcraft, that's what it is. Look at me, so sick I can't stand up, and what else could it be, I ask you?'

Alicia had worked herself into a veritable frenzy, shaking her head to and fro and thumping the bed with her fist. Alarmed, Jennifer tried to calm her.

'Perhaps if you were just outside occasionally,' she suggested, 'in the sunshine and the fresh air. I don't think it could be good for anyone to confine herself indefinitely. Even my mother . . . '

Alicia seemed not to have heard her at all but rather appeared to be contemplating some dark inner voices of her own. Suddenly she interrupted Jennifer.

'Call Walter.' Alicia screamed, turning livid. 'Now, at once! I want to see him.'

Jennifer's face burned at being treated so rudely but she was too well disciplined herself to argue further. Without a further word she went to the library, where she had seen Walter a short time before.

'Your wife wishes to speak to you,' she informed him curtly.

He gave her a surprised look, studying her face, which only served to heighten her color and further disconcert her.

At length he rose from his chair and went swiftly along the hall to his wife's bedroom, his long strides easily leaving Jennifer behind, so that by the time she arrived at the bedroom and went in, Alicia was already unleashing an angry torrent of words aimed at her husband.

'She has got to leave,' Alicia was saying, her voice rising hysterically until she was all but screaming. 'She must go.'

Walter's normal speaking voice sounded like a whisper in contrast to Alicia's shouting. 'I can't just turn her out,' he said.

'I won't have her here.'

'You're working yourself up over

nothing.' Despite the softness of his voice, Walter spoke with firm determination.

'I tell you, she's killing me. She's a witch, like her mother, and she's killing me with her tricks. And you don't even care. No one cares if I die or not.'

'That's not true.' Walter went to the bed and knelt, trying to take her in his arms and comfort her.

'Leave me alone,' she shrieked, slapping his hands away. 'I believe you want her to kill me. You want me dead. That's why you brought that witch into the house.'

She gave a sharp gasp, clutching at her breast and threw her head back with a grimace of pain.

To Jennifer, standing helping just inside the door, it certainly looked as if Alicia's pain was real — or was this just more of her acting? She went swiftly to her. She had to fight an increasing dislike for this cruel, grasping woman who could be so venomous toward a mere child and so heartless toward a patient and gentle husband, but she could not let this scene continue, and not for Alicia's sake alone.

'Mrs. Dere, let me help you,' she said, putting an arm around the woman's stiff shoulders. Alicia did not resist, but sank weakly into Jennifer's arms. Jennifer looked past her, directly at Walter. Their eyes met and for a moment it seemed as if they shared some secret knowledge, as if in some odd way the two of them were united in purpose against his wife.

She was suddenly angry, angry that she should be thrust into that position between them, angry that she should share his thoughts regarding his wife. Angry that his wife should join them together in understanding.

'Perhaps you should leave us,' she said to him coldly, because she was angry, and frightened, too, but she did not watch him go. She gave her attention instead to the woman in her arms. Alicia was weeping softly now, as helpless as a kitten. It was hard to believe that a moment before she had shown the savagery of a jungle cat.

For just a moment before he left, Walter paused, looking down at the two women — at his wife, so shrill, so hard and demanding, who had brought so much unhappiness into his life — and at Jennifer, so unbelievably lovely, so soft and gentle.

He knew then why he had felt distracted these last few days, unable to eat right or sleep right, and forgetting things. At the same time, though, he had felt all charged up, recklessly alive. He had caught himself laughing. *Caught* himself, because it was something he did so rarely anymore, and he had more energy and strength than a child.

Always, something seemed to be on the tip of his tongue, hanging around the corners of his mind. He would be reading and he would think of her, and he would come to the doorway to look at her, not really thinking anything, not consciously, only looking as if at some marvel, as if at a miracle. Each time she had seemed new and wonderful and mysterious to him, and something within him had quickened and stirred, and he had come away more puzzled than before, and more alive too.

Now he knew. He was in love.

From the first she had frightened him,

with those wide, vulnerable eyes of hers and that tremulous smile that tried so hard to be brave. That first day, he had looked at her standing in the door of the station, and he had known that she dared not come to Darkwater, not only because of what Alicia would say.

He knew his wife would be furious, but instinct had warned him of some greater threat and he had not been wise enough to understand the warning. Now it was too late. He was like a man who, so long as no food was put before him, was not hungry, but now there was a banquet set within his sight and hunger gnawed at his innards.

He went out of the bedroom, angry with himself to discover that his hand was shaking as he pulled the door closed. His mother was in the hall. Alicia's screaming had been audible all over the house.

'It's all right,' he said. 'Miss Hale is with her and she seems to be quieting down.'

His mother's eyes searched his face and she had a look of alarm in her eyes that was not entirely for Alicia's outburst.

They knew each other well, mother and son, and just as she had glanced at his face and divined his inner turmoil, so now he understood at once the reason for the concern he saw on her face.

'Is it so obvious, then?' he asked.

She did not answer him, but studied his face for a moment. When finally she did speak, it had nothing to do with that.

'I'll see if Miss Hale needs help,' she said.

'Yes, please do that.'

He went to the library and closed the door and sank into one of the big chairs there as if in a fit of exhaustion. He leaned forward, burying his face in his hands.

How had he come to this? He was not a philanderer by nature. He did not love his wife. He was honest enough with himself to admit that, but he had always been as good a husband as he knew how to be. Despite all of her jealous ravings, he had never given her any reason to distrust him. Always he had honored the marriage vows, to the best of his abilities, even when she had not. Had she not promised to love? And to honor?

It had been intended once that Walter would become a Baptist preacher like his father. That had been his father's fervent wish and if his mother did not share the fervor, she happily acquiesced in the plans.

Walter, too, seemed to agree, and he even began study for the ministry. Everyone 'knew' that Walter would be the finest preacher in the South. It did not matter that it was not so lucrative a calling. Melvin Dere, Walter's father, had married Helen Oglethorpe, and she had come to him a woman of considerable wealth. Melvin's zeal for his calling had not prevented his wise husbandry of her wealth. Walter would never need to worry about making a decent living.

It was not that which worried Walter. What bothered him was something else, something far more fundamental. It was the quickening of his spirits when he heard a song, or saw a flower, or when he read the poems of Shakespeare. It was the throbbing of his pulse that bothered him when a pretty girl went by, and the delight he took the first time he kissed one of those pretty girls and knew he would have to do more than kiss.

A wonderful joy of life ran in his veins. He loved the things of the earth, perhaps too much, When he listed to the mockingbird and smelled the sweet aroma of the honeysuckle, he knew he could never excoriate others for their sins without his being a hypocrite, and he had informed his father that he was going to run the plantation instead of becoming a preacher.

A violent quarrel had ensued, through which Walter had remained firm in his purpose, but the disappointment had been a grave shock to his father, who was already ill, and he had taken to his bed.

That stern old Puritan had looked around for some means of bringing his son back to the religion he feared Walter had abandoned. He had long thought of a marriage between Walter and Alicia Longstreet. She was fiercely religious already at her young age, a few years older than Walter, and one of the pillars of the church.

Walter was plagued with guilt that he had caused his father's illness. When his father asked him to promise to marry Alicia Longstreet, he had agreed gladly. Why should he not? She was young and pretty, everyone said she was an angel. He was virile, a young man ready for a wife, prepared to be a good husband. They were married and only a few days afterward, assured that he had saved his son's soul, Melvin Dere died.

He died without ever knowing what a tragic mistake the wedding had been for his son. Alicia was indeed a 'good' woman, too good to be a real wife. She clung tenaciously to everything in the church doctrine that was harsh and repressive and rejected anything that was soft. Love, in her vocabulary, referred to her feeling for the Lord, not to any feeling for her husband. As for him, she had married him to save his soul, and she meant to do that if she had to make his life a hell in order to prepare him for heaven.

Walter knew on their wedding night that he had made a mistake. He, whose blood ran hot in his splendid young body, clasped a woman of ice in his arms and was unable to melt her.

'You are behaving like an animal,' she complained.

'I am your husband,' he argued.

But for all her coldness, Alicia knew of a woman's obligations to her husband and her marriage. With the sanctity of a martyr, she permitted her husband to perform his duties. In due time, little Mary was born. Peter was born almost three years later.

When, not so much later this time, Alicia informed her husband that she would once again permit his attentions, it was she who was disappointed. Disappointed because somehow in performing her 'obligation,' and despite her frigid nature, she had discovered some source of passion within her that responded to her husband's attention.

Now, however, it was Walter who denied, who informed her that he would make no further demands upon her of that nature. He said it was out of consideration for her health. In fact, it disgusted him to hold that coldness in his arms and to be made to feel guilty for responding to the natural urge within him.

Passion was like a seed that had been planted within her, that grew and grew and sent out tendrils, seeking a sun that could no longer shine for her. In time, those vines and tendrils began to strangle her . . . and their marriage.

If she had been able to manage it, they would have strangled Walter as well.

4

Jennifer woke with a strange sense of unfamiliarity. She did not know where she was or why. Then as sleep fell away from her and she sat up looking around, she realized she was in Alicia's room.

Alicia's 'spell' had lasted well into the night. Each time Jennifer made as if to go, thinking that Alicia was at last asleep, the older woman sat up, crying and begging Jennifer not to leave her.

'You don't know what nightmares I have,' she sobbed. 'It's that girl, she sends them, I know she does. I just know it. I used to sleep like an angel and now I dare not close my eyes or the demons are here tormenting me.'

So Jennifer had stayed, sitting in the chair by the bed, and at last they had both slept. Now it was morning, the pale sunlight filtering through the curtains, making motes of dust dance in the golden stream.

Jennifer stood and stretched. She felt stiff from sleeping in the hard chair. She looked down at Alicia, now deep asleep. In repose she looked so much younger, so gentle and . . . yes, even angelic. It was hard to imagine that face, which looked pretty when still, could become so ugly and twisted with anger and violent passion.

Suddenly Jennifer felt the need to be away from this emotion-charged room, this troubled woman, away from her own troubled thoughts, even. She let herself quietly out of the room, moving noiselessly along the hall, to the back door.

Outside it was cool with the night's lingering coolness. The day's heat was just beginning to descend, like a warm blanket. The grass was still damp with dew and she lifted her skirt slightly to spare the hem. The magnolia trees dripped with their fragrant blossoms and a lark greeted the day with joyous song.

The house and the entire plantation, with the sweeping green lawns and the wide, carefully cultivated fields of cotton and cane, looked as if they had been dropped from above, into the very heart of the bayou. They had been wrested from the swamp and the swamp stood vigilantly nearby, as if waiting to reclaim them.

'Hello,' a voice said behind her. She turned to find Liza standing nearby.

'What are you doing out so early?' Jennifer asked.

'I was about to ask you the same thing. I always get up early. There's no one to yell at me and tell me I'm doing everything wrong.'

Jennifer felt a wave of sympathy for this girl, a mere child, actually, who had somehow become the object of an emotional tug-of-war between a man and his wife. If only she had been able to establish a friendship with the girl — but Liza had steadfastly held her at arm's length, although there was no open antagonism between them. The fact was, Liza had no interest in anyone but Walter. For Liza none of the others, herself included, really existed.

'Yes, I can understand the need to be alone sometimes,' Jennifer said. 'I feel that myself. That's what I am doing out so early.'

'When I want to be by myself, I go into the bayou.'

Jennifer glanced past her, at the swamp forest that here edged its way almost up to the house. The thick trees with their lush growth provided a green wall that blocked any view of the swamp. She had an impression of vividly colored flowers and exotic blossoms, of hanging moss and thick vines like snakes, and tall marsh grass. It looked dark and luxuriant and mysterious.

'Isn't it dangerous to wander into the swamp?'

'Not if you stay on the paths. If you follow that path right there,' Liza pointed to a worn trail that went past the outbuildings, 'and when it forks, stay to the right, it will bring you back here directly. It's a very pretty walk.'

Jennifer suddenly felt the desire to surrender herself to that green darkness. 'Would you like to walk with me?'

'No, you go ahead. You did say you wanted to be alone, didn't you?'

Although she had not said that exactly, Jennifer did feel like being alone. She was surprised at Liza's perception.

'Yes, I think I do,' she said aloud. 'If anyone asks, I will be back soon.'

She set out, leisurely following the path as Liza had indicated. Once she glanced back over her shoulder and saw Liza still standing in the same spot, staring after her. She waved, and Liza waved back.

A moment later, the swamp had swallowed her up.

★   ★   ★

From the window of the kitchen, a worried Bess watched Jennifer disappear into the swamp.

'That's not good,' she said to herself. 'That is no place for her.'

For a moment she wondered if she should say something to someone else in the house — Mr. Walter, for instance.

She liked the new girl. Like everyone else, Bess had to suffer Alicia's sharp tongue from time to time, but with a difference. The others could say something back if they wanted. Not that they ever did, but they knew that they could. It rankled with Bess to still be treated like a slave — like the Deres had never treated their slaves. And by a woman who had no right.

But the new girl had stood up for her. Alicia had spoken sharp to her one day when the lunch Bess had brought in was not as hot as she seemed to think it ought to be.

'You're stupid, that's the trouble,' Alicia had almost shouted at her. 'No white person would serve food this way.'

'I've never noticed that any race had a monopoly on stupidity,' Jennifer had said, very quietly but very cuttingly.

'Wait until you have spent a little more time with our blacks,' Alice said scornfully.

'They are no longer 'your' blacks,' Jennifer said. 'They are free now.'

To Bess's surprise, Alicia had said nothing in reply and had concentrated instead on eating the soup that a minute before had been too cold for her. Of course, Bess herself said nothing but she had admired the new girl for standing up to Alicia, as the others usually did not.

Now, she wondered why she was going into the swamp, but she was in the process of making candles and if she stopped the wax would harden and she would have to start over.

She decided to see if Miss Jennifer did not get back all right, and if she didn't return by the time Bess was finished with her candles, then she would tell someone else.

★ ★ ★

It was amazing, Jennifer thought, how very thick the growth was. Certainly there was nothing like this in the woods of Tennessee. Although daylight outside, in here it was nearly dark.

The thick trees blotted out the sun and created a warm, damp and musty smelling gloom. The leaves stirred and rustled, moved by unfelt breezes or perhaps by the movements of birds and animals. All about was thick vegetation and profuse flowers such as she had never seen before, and the huge trunks of trees entwined with clinging vines.

The path that she followed, however, was wide and worn smooth, and easy to follow. She looked to the right and down, and realized that only a few feet from the path the land swooped downward and was covered with water that gleamed darkly in the semi-gloom and was thick with tall grasses.

A careless traveler could wander from the path and suddenly be in water knee-deep or even deeper. There was no telling how deep that water was, nor what lay beneath the brackish surface.

She thought of traveling this path at night. For that you would need a sure knowledge of the lay of the land. Certainly now she would be careful to stay on the path. Once she thought she heard someone call and she paused to listen, but it did not come again and she decided she had imagined it. Or maybe it had been a bird, she told herself, and went on.

She came to a fork in the path, with a

trail going off in each direction. 'Stay to the right,' Liza had told her. She veered to the right.

This path was narrow and not as well worn. In places the grasses and the vines clung to her skirt, and the low hanging branches ran leafy fingers across her cheek.

I won't go much further, she told herself, still confident that she was in no danger of getting lost. Liza had told her that the path would eventually lead her back, but she did not want to face too long a walk home.

The walk had served one purpose, though. She felt calmer than before. Here in the swamp, cut off from the sight of other people, from any sound of civilization, she felt truly alone and as if her problems were distant. She took her thoughts out as she would take clothes from a trunk, shaking them and holding them at arm's length to examine them.

Driven by necessity, she had come to this little backwater town expecting to be nurse to an ill woman. Instead she found herself part time companion to a woman who, so far as she could see, had nothing wrong with her physically but who was insanely possessive of her husband.

But was she being quite fair? Alicia's problems seemed mostly to be more hysteria than anything else, but at other times, it did seem as if she were in actual pain. Or could the mind simply play that kind of trick on the body. She wasn't educated enough to know the answer to that.

As for Walter . . . if only her heartbeat did not quicken when their eyes met. If only she did not thrill so to the sight of him, to the sound of his voice. He was only a man, after all, and not the first one she had ever met. She'd had a beau, whom she had fully intended to marry, had he only come back from the war.

And there was another soldier, a gallant young defender of the Confederacy, who had come back and she had dressed his physical wounds and tried to salve the other, deeper ones.

And a Northerner briefly, arrogant, cocksure . . . but what did any of that matter now? She was here, and Walter

Dere was married, however unhappily.

Did she only imagine that light she saw in his eyes when he looked at her? Or did he feel something for her, too?

'And if he does?' she asked herself crossly, 'what good could ever come of it?'

Perhaps she ought to go away from here, leave Darkwater and the temptation that he had come to represent. Perhaps, if she did not guard her thoughts and her actions very carefully, if she should ever give into the wild desire that had begun to tremble within her at the mere sight of him — why then there would be shame and great unhappiness for everyone.

It was no use to tell herself how it had all come about. Her loneliness after her mother's death, her feeling of desolation. Caring for her mother these last few years had left her no time for romance. Perhaps, looking back, she would have been wiser to have become that Northerner's mistress as he had so obviously wanted. Money would not then have been the problem it had become for her, that had driven her here.

All of that was behind her, though. She

was hundreds of miles from home, with no ties, no responsibilities except to herself. She had met a man, handsome, soft-spoken, intelligent, who shared her love of books, with whom she could discuss things. A man of strength and purpose. For the first time she felt the desire to be able to lean on someone else, she on whom others had always leaned. Suddenly she wanted to be a woman, and belong to a man. She was tired of being strong, of being wise, and most especially of being independent.

But she could never give in to the urge she had begun to feel, to put herself in his arms, to lean her head against his powerful chest, and abandon herself to his will, however briefly. They were wicked thoughts, but she could not help thinking them.

Suddenly the path she had been following widened into a clearing. Here the trees did not meet overhead. She could see the sky, blue and deep, and the hot sunlight fell in a golden cascade. A dragonfly darted past her face, gleaming green and silver.

She paused for a moment, and was surprised to discover she was not alone. Since entering the swamp she had seen no one nor even heard the sound of a voice, so it was something of a shock to see a woman standing not far away. She was withered and very old looking and barefoot, her toes with their long, yellowed nails looking like the talons of some bird of prey. Her gray hair was tied up in a bandanna, the way the blacks used to do at home and her dress was little more than a rag.

At the moment she was bent over with her back to Jennifer, gathering some sort of herb from beneath a spreading tree. She had not yet become aware of Jennifer's presence. Had she been able to, Jennifer would have gone on without intruding, but the path went directly by where the old crone was kneeling.

'Good morning,' Jennifer said to be polite.

The reaction to her simple greeting was swift and startling. The woman leapt about with amazing agility for one so obviously old. Plainly the unexpected sound of a voice had alarmed her, but what was especially surprising to Jennifer was that the woman seemed angered as well. The look she gave Jennifer was threatening.

'Who are you?' she demanded, her eyes gleaming with a dark light. 'What are you doing here?'

'Why, I . . . ' Jennifer was astonished by this unfriendly behavior. 'I am Jennifer Hale. I am from Darkwater, and I was just taking a walk . . . '

'You were spying on me,' the old woman said in a savage whisper. 'You were trying to see what herbs I pick for my potion.'

'No.' Jennifer was not only bewildered but actually frightened by the woman's wild manner. 'I was quite surprised to see you here, in fact. I thought I was alone, you see, and then when I saw you . . . '

'I've warned everyone.' She came closer with a threatening look on her face. 'Warned them and warned them. My secrets are my own. No one can steal them from me. I'll kill anyone who tries to steal them.'

'I have not tried to steal your secrets, whatever they are,' Jennifer said, indignation momentarily overcoming her fear. 'I have no interest in them, or in you.''

'Liar.' The woman suddenly raised her large walking stick as if she would strike Jennifer with it.

Alarmed, Jennifer tried to step backward but her foot caught on a vine and to her horror she went sprawling into the mud and the tall grass alongside the path. Her hand came down in the greenish-black water of the swamp.

'Sneaking around, spying on me, I'll teach you,' the crone shouted, striking out at Jennifer with her stick. Her blow was wild and the stick struck the ground instead, an inch or two from Jennifer's face. Jennifer screamed in terror.

'Don't,' she cried, but the woman raised the stick to strike at her again.

'Think you're so clever, sneaking around, sneaking up on people . . . '

Desperately Jennifer kicked out with her foot. Her skirts prevented her from kicking with any real force, but it was enough to trip her attacker. The crone stumbled too and fell into the muddy grass alongside Jennifer.

Jennifer was young and agile and in a moment she had managed to scramble to her feet. She ran away before the old woman had recovered herself, along the path and back the way she had come, holding her skirts high. She sobbed and gasped as she ran. She had never suffered such a senseless attack before, not even in the heat of the war.

She came around a turning in the path and gave a little cry of alarm as she saw there was someone in the path, directly in front of her. He was too close and she was running too fast to avoid him.

She was in his arms before she realized it was Walter. Not even thinking of what was right or wrong, she threw herself against him, sobbing into his chest.

'What is it, what happened?' he demanded, holding her close.

'An old woman. She tried to hit me with a stick,' Jennifer sobbed.

'Mrs. Hodges! Wait here, I'll go . . . '

'No.' She grabbed his arm and, taking a deep breath, managed to quiet her sobs.

'I'm all right now, truly I am. She did not harm me, she only frightened me.'

'She didn't strike you?' he demanded, looking down into her face anxiously.

'No. She swung at me with her stick, but I don't know if she really meant to hit me or if she was just trying to frighten me. Truly, I am all right. I was just terrified, that's all.'

She suddenly thought of how she must look and gave a little laugh. 'I am a sight, though,' Her dress, already wrinkled from a night of sleeping in Alicia's chair, was even more so by now, and it was also torn slightly and stained from grass and mud. Her hair lay in damp strands and she knew there was mud on her face as well as on her hands.

'I think you look very beautiful,' he said in a changed voice. 'I think you would always look very beautiful no matter what the circumstances.'

Her heart skipped a beat as she looked up into his face, so near her own. Only a few minutes before she had been thinking of him, of his dark eyes boring into hers, of his strong arms, that now held her close.

For a moment neither of them spoke. She could not. She could only feel as if she were fainting, her legs going weak. She stared with wide eyes as his face came closer, closer, his lips parting to close over hers. His countenance blurred as he came too near to see him clearly, and she could only feel the heat of his body, the power of his arms locked tight about her, and his own heart pounding against her breast in a crescendo that matched her own.

Suddenly the world, that had faded from them, came back to her in a rush, and she cried, 'No,' and turned her face away, so that his lips only brushed her cheek.

The moment was gone. His arms grew slack and fell away from her. She swayed as if she would fall, but she caught herself and stood firm.

'I think we had better go back,' she said, her voice quavering.

'Of course.' He took her arm again, but this time it was only a polite gesture, to help her onto the path. She went by him and began to retrace her route.

Because the silence between them grew so heavy, she asked, 'How did you happen to come this way, anyway?'

'I was looking for you. I looked out the window and saw you, and then when I came outside later, you were gone. I asked Liza what had happened to you and she said you had gone into the swamp, so I came after you right away. You really should have been warned, it is not safe to be wandering around in here by yourself.'

'But Liza assured me it was quite safe.'

He smiled indulgently. 'I suppose in her mind it is. She has lived in the swamp and she knows it like the back of her hand. She just didn't think that it would be different for you. I will speak to her about that.'

But as she walked the narrow path, Jennifer found herself remembering how confidently Liza had reassured her, and she recalled Liza standing looking after her, lifting her hand to wave.

Had she meant that gesture to be a last goodbye?

Jennifer was surprised to learn that her taking a stroll had caused considerable excitement. When she and Walter returned to the house, Helen and Bess were waiting in the yard. They looked Jennifer over as she walked up, as if expecting to find limbs missing.

'Liza told us you were in the swamp and that Walter had gone looking for you,' Helen said. 'Are you all right? You look a fright.'

'I am all right,' Jennifer said, trying to make light of the incident. She found she could not look directly at Walter's mother without a sensation of guilt. 'I took a fall trying to get away from some mad old woman with a stick who accused me of spying on her.'

'Mrs. Hodges,' Walter said in a grim voice.

'The swamp witch,' Bess murmured.

'Thank God I came along when I did,' Walter added. 'There's no telling what she might do when she's riled up.'

'And she is only one of the swamp's

dangers,' Helen said as they came into the kitchen. 'You must be wary of going there alone.'

'Only us local people go into the swamp,' Bess said. 'Me, I know what to expect, and no self-respecting snake would bite me anyway.' Her comment made the others smile and some of the tension in the air was dissipated.

Even as she was speaking, though, Bess watched the others with a keen eye. She looked from Jennifer's face, where not even the mud smeared across it could hide her confusion, to Walter's, that glowed with a new, inner light, and she knew without a doubt that these two were in love, although maybe they did not yet know it themselves.

And Lord knows, he deserves some happiness, Bess thought. Aloud, she said, 'I better fix you some tea. What are you doing out anyway without having had a decent breakfast?'

'I think I would like to change into a clean dress and freshen up a bit,' Jennifer said.

'You go right ahead, dear,' Helen said.

'And you never mind about the children today. You've had quite enough to do staying with Alicia all night. A day off won't hurt and the children will probably enjoy a holiday.'

'I don't want to set the children a bad example.'

'I'll hear no more about it,' Helen insisted. 'Go on, clean up now, and come back down and Bess will give you a real breakfast.'

Jennifer did as she was ordered and Walter left the kitchen in her wake. As they went out, Bess and Helen exchanged glances. They had known one another many years. Each of them knew just what the other was thinking.

★   ★   ★

When Jennifer came downstairs a short time later, the others were waiting breakfast for her in the dining room.

By now the memory of Jennifer's experience with Mrs. Hodges in the swamp was receding. She could even chide herself for being driven to panic by an old woman whom she ought to have been able to manage.

As for her other experience in the swamp, with Walter, that seemed even more portentous. She had come so close to kissing him! And she knew that once she had allowed such feelings to be expressed, there would be no turning back from shame and tragedy. How had she come so far, come to feel so much, in so short a time?

She would thrust him from her mind, except in his role as her employer and Alicia's husband. She would not even give love an opportunity to take root and flourish in her heart. Surely that was better than the alternative.

When she came into the dining room, however, and saw the way his eyes sought hers at once, her resolve threatened to crumble and she felt herself tremble slightly.

She soon found that Walter did not look back upon the business with Mrs. Hodges as lightly as she did. When she had greeted the others and taken her place at the table, he rose and excused himself for a moment, leaving the room. He was back almost at once, with Liza in tow.

'Miss Jennifer had some difficulty in the swamp,' he said to Liza. 'As it has turned out, she was not hurt, but she might very well have been. She could have walked into the sand and been swallowed up forever, she might have met a snake or tripped or fallen and hurt herself. Or Mrs. Hodges might have actually hurt her instead of just scaring her.'

Liza said nothing. Her eyes were downcast and there was a sullen look on her face that Jennifer had come to recognize from their lessons.

Yet if you did not look closely, she would seem to be quite chagrined by the whole thing. Jennifer wondered briefly if Walter had come to recognize and understand that look, or was his affection for the child so strong as to blind his otherwise keen perception?

'There really was no harm done,' Jennifer said, because it was plain to her at least that Liza did not intend to make any reply. 'I let myself be frightened rather too easily.'

Jennifer felt genuinely sorry for the girl, despite her failure to establish a friendship with her. Liza was the object of so much disapproving adult attention, and so often the victim of Alicia's temper. Nor did the usually loving natures of Bess and Helen respond to the child's desire for affection, because they both saw Liza as a problem in the house, a cause of Alicia's 'spells' and Walter's further harassment.

'The point is not whether you were hurt or not,' Walter said. 'You might have been seriously hurt, and it would have been at least partly Liza's fault. You did tell Miss Jennifer it would be safe for her to go into the swamp, did you not?'

'I go there all the time,' Liza said in sudden defiance, looking up at him. Her eyes flashed with youthful anger, but Jennifer detected what was below the surface of that anger — a silent plea for Walter's understanding.

Perhaps he saw it too, for when he spoke again he sounded less angry. 'But you are used to it. It was careless of you

114

not to remember that Miss Jennifer is a stranger here and unaware of the dangers.'

He paused and when there was no reply forthcoming, he said, 'You will have to apologize.'

For a long moment the girl struggled with herself. Then at last she looked directly at Jennifer. 'I am sorry,' she said simply.

Jennifer was shocked. Although the words were delivered in a colorless monotone, Liza's face was turned so that only Jennifer saw it directly. What she saw was a look of utter hatred. Liza was furious with her, and in a flash she realized it was because of Liza's deep attachment to Walter and her feeling that Jennifer was somehow responsible for Walter's present displeasure with her.

Jennifer recovered herself quickly, though, and as the others were waiting in silence, she said, 'I accept your apology, and I think the less to-do we have over this in the future, the better for all.'

But Jennifer knew that between her and Liza passed a strange antagonism that she did not fully understand. It was as if in that moment the two of them were locked in combat, with Walter as the prize.

What fanciful nonsense, Jennifer told herself when the family's attention was finally returned to their breakfast. As if Walter belonged to either of us, which he does not and cannot. He is married to Alicia, and I have no claim on him, and Liza is only a child with a child's adulation of someone who has protected her.

Yet when she again saw Liza that morning, disappearing down the hall, she had once more that strange feeling of a contest between them.

Since she had been firmly excused from teaching this morning, she went to look in on Alicia. She found the convalescent sitting up in bed and looking more alert than she had in days.

'Good morning,' Jennifer greeted her. 'It is a very pretty day, isn't it?'

'Is it?' Alicia asked, narrowing her eyes. 'I heard you had some difficulty already this morning.'

'Nothing of any consequence,' Jennifer

said, wondering how on earth Alicia had managed to learn of this morning's business.

Alicia was not to be put off that easily, though. With one birdlike hand she seized Jennifer's wrist so tightly that it hurt.

'I want to hear all about it,' she said in a fierce whisper.

Jennifer told her what had happened, minimizing as much as possible the danger, and especially the import of the scene between her and Walter. Alicia, however, for all her possessiveness and her shrewdness, seemed entirely uninterested in Walter's role in the proceedings. She was concerned with Liza and, to Jennifer's surprise, with Mrs. Hodges.

'That's her,' Alicia said, her head bobbing furiously. 'The swamp witch. It's her mother.'

'I don't understand.'

'Mrs. Hodges. She is Liza's mother.'

'No,' Jennifer said, stunned. She thought of the vicious old crone in the swamp. It was impossible to believe that she could be the mother of anyone as young and pretty as Liza.

Yet, Peter had said the same thing. And Liza had reacted with a violence too strong for ordinary childhood teasing.

'It's true,' Alicia said. 'She is the swamp witch, that's how everybody around here knows her. She has lived in a shack in the swamp as long as anyone remembers, since long before the war. She brews all sorts of vile potions and works spells. There's some as has gone to her for help with their problems, but I call that the devil's work, not the sort of thing a good Christian would get into.'

'Surely you don't mean that literally. You can't believe she is truly a witch.'

'But I do. It is her magic that is killing me. Hers and Liza's, and that's who Liza learned it from.' For a moment her face looked so ghastly that Jennifer felt a little shiver of alarm travel her spine.

'I didn't think anyone in this modern day and age really believed in witches,' Jennifer said with a smile, trying to make light of the subject.

'That's because you have not read your Bible fully. Remember Luke, 8:2 . . . 'And certain women, which had been healed of evil spirits and infirmities, Mary, called Magdalene, out of whom went seven devils . . . ' Now, do you believe what the Bible says?'

'Yes, but not always literally. Devils, as referred to in the Bible, often meant epilepsy, and you certainly do not believe Liza is an epileptic.'

'What about the witch of Endor?'

'She was a medium. And I have not heard that Liza communicates with the dead.'

'I wouldn't be surprised,' Alicia said with a disgruntled look. 'She's always up to some tricks. Once she pulled an apple out of Walter's hat when he had just taken it off his head, and he swore there hadn't been anything in it.'

'Why, that's just sleight-of-hand. How wonderful. I for one would like to see her do some of her tricks, and I am sure it will be seen to be only trickery and not magic. But I wonder how she learned them. Is she really Mrs. Hodges' daughter?'

'Yes. Walter came in one night, over a year ago, with this ragged bundle in his arms. He said he had found Mrs. Hodges beating her and he had taken the girl away from her, and she was going to stay here until he could find her a home.'

'Perhaps he has not been able to find anyone to take in an orphan. Since the war, so many people have been left destitute in the South.'

'But there are people who would take her,' Alicia said bitterly. 'The Woodbirds said they would take her to work. They needed a girl, but he won't send her over there.'

Jennifer thought she knew why. She had seen plenty of girls in the last few years who, poverty-stricken, had to go into servitude. She knew how cruelly they were often treated, sometimes far worse than the blacks had been treated before the war, and all so they could earn a place to sleep in an attic and a meal a day. No, Walter would not want to commit a child, any child, to that if he could help it.

'She is a witch,' Alicia went on, speaking in a monotone, as if she had said all this often before. 'She has him bewitched. He thinks more of her than he does his own children. Why, he thinks more of her than he does of me.'

Jennifer smiled to herself at this comment, which she felt sure went to the heart of the matter. Jealousy was a poison, but she did not say this aloud.

'And I have been sick ever since she came,' Alicia concluded.

'I think you are sick because you do not eat properly, and you spend all your time in bed. The blood has no opportunity to circulate if you are not moving about a little. That is the latest medical opinion in Memphis, at any rate, and I think you could do with some fresh air and some sunshine. I wish you would let me arrange for you to spend some time outside, on the porch, perhaps. It is quite warm now and I don't think there could be any danger.'

Alicia sank back upon her pillow, looking gloomy. 'I'm not well enough to go outside.'

Jennifer shrugged. 'Very well, but you cannot continue to blame Liza for an illness you will do nothing to mitigate.'

Alicia gave her an angry look. 'You

think I'm crazy. They all think I'm crazy, but wait, you will see. The time will come.'

Outside in the hall, Jennifer paused to consider what she'd been told. Liza, the daughter of Mrs. Hodges, that vicious creature in the swamp? And she, Mrs. Hodges, was regarded locally as a witch. It was no wonder that Alicia credited Liza with using magic.

5

Helen had made plans to go into the town of Durieville and she suggested that Jennifer come with her.

'We'll both go, in the trap,' Helen said, enthused by the idea of an outing. 'I have several things I want to shop for and it will give you an opportunity to look over the town. Not that there's so much to see, but still . . . '

'All right,' Jennifer said, pleased at a chance to take a vacation from Darkwater. Perhaps away from the house, and from Walter, things might seem a little clearer to her.

It was a fine day for a drive. When Jennifer had made this trip before, the night Walter picked her up at the station, it had been pouring rain and she had seen little but water. Now she could see that it was a lovely drive. The bayous, dark and mysterious, stretched from the side of the road into the distance, with the flash of colors from the many flowers, the calls of exotic birds, and the warm breeze that ruffled her hair.

Helen was a fine driver, handling the horses with the easy skill of long familiarity. She was good company too, chatting about people in the neighborhood and myriad trivial matters. She barely touched upon any of the problems at Darkwater — Alicia's illness, Walter's preoccupation (could she know the cause of it, Jennifer wondered for a brief, awful moment?) or Liza's unwelcome presence. By the time they had reached the town of Durieville, Jennifer too had all but forgotten Darkwater's problems and the unpleasant beginning to her morning.

Durieville was a town serving the needs of the nearby plantation owners, and had really no other reason to exist. But it was a pretty little town, seen in the golden light of this early summer afternoon.

This bayou part of Louisiana — or Lusianne, as the natives called it — was all marsh and woods and greenery, with spots of open water, lakes and streams, looking like they had been punched out of the green in random pattern. The water lay deep and gleaming, with the greenery pushed right up to its edges. There was some land, most of it flat but with a few gently rolling hills, where the forests had been cut away and only a low brush grew.

And of course there were the swamps, choked with reeds and cattails and marsh grass, so that you could not say for sure where the land ended and the water began.

Durieville lay as if some giant hand had held a fistful of buildings and thrown them to the ground in a haphazard pattern. They lay drawn together as they might have done if magnetized, the biggest toward the center in thick clusters and the smaller buildings scattered sparsely outward. There were none of the neat squares and corners to be found in cities planned by men.

Entering down the road from the bayou, one drifted between green banks for a mile or more before, coming down a gentle incline, one began to see the buildings that lay thin at the edge of town.

At the foot of this incline the road, straight until now, twisted around the white-painted Baptist Church, which sat directly in its path. Past the church, the road went straight a bit more before turning again, this time around the train station.

Beyond the station was the town hall, a neo-classic building that looked pretentious for such an unimportant town. It was shaded with magnolia trees and a big oak dripping with moss. The road passed the schoolhouse, where the town's poorer children had their lessons. It was a ramshackle looking wooden building in need of paint, with no playground but a dirt yard in the back. The Deres, of course, did not send their children to the school and if they had, the children in attendance would have been shocked.

Past the school lay the town's 'business district,' a short street of storefronts where the local people did what shopping they had to do between trips to Shreveport or New Orleans, where they made their major purchases.

'What a pretty little town,' Jennifer said

when Helen had parked the trap along the main street.

'Do you think so?' Helen glanced along the street as if seeing it for the first time. 'I suppose it is. One gets used to seeing it. Like the face of someone you know well. It is too familiar to know if it is handsome or not.'

Jennifer thought, I would always know that Walter was handsome, but she pushed that thought roughly from her mind and looked again along the way they had come. Traveling through the South, on her way here, she had gotten used to seeing towns that had been desolated and were not yet rebuilt. It seemed there was hardly a town without some buildings in ruins, blackened boards and broken windows testifying to the slow end of the war.

Here, though, there was no sign of war, nothing to indicate that a nation had been at death grips with itself a few years before. There was only the quaintly twisting main street running under thick lush trees, the coziness and the charm, the rich green and the warm, scented breeze from the bayou.

'I want to look for some material from the Emporium,' Helen said, lifting her skirts above the dust of the street. 'And there are some things we need for the kitchen. I'll get them at the general store. Do you want to walk along with me or do you have some errands of your own?'

Jennifer hesitated for a moment. Something had occurred to her earlier, although this was the first opportunity she'd had to act upon it.

'As a matter of fact there is something I want to do,' she said. 'I wonder if you could tell me where to find the doctor?'

'Doctor Goodman? Why, his office is just over there, you can see it from here, with the shingle hanging above the door. But there isn't anything wrong, is there?' She looked suddenly concerned.

'No, nothing at all is wrong with me, I'm fine, really I am,' Jennifer said, laying a gloved hand on Helen's arm. 'It's only that, so long as I am acting as a nurse to Alicia, I thought I might talk to him about her condition. Perhaps he can give me some suggestions for caring for her.'

'I see. Of course.' Helen looked so unconvinced, however, that Jennifer felt constrained to add a further remark.

'I often consulted with the doctor over my mother's condition.'

'There's no need for you to trouble yourself, really. I've talked to Doctor Goodman often about Alicia. But if it will make you feel better, by all means drop in on him. You will find him a bit absentminded in some ways, but quite competent. Ask him if he will join us for dinner tomorrow evening.'

Helen left her then, after again ascertaining that Jennifer knew which of the stores she would be in. Jennifer made her own way across the street, smiling at a group of children playing in the street, who stared wide-eyed at her as she passed. She guessed that the Deres were objects of awe here in Durieville, and that made her an object of no small curiosity herself.

She had scarcely banged the knocker on the door of the doctor's house before the door was yanked open. The inside was so dark in contrast to the harsh glare outside that for a moment Jennifer could not see in.

'Yes, what is it?' a gruff voice asked.

When Jennifer eye's had adjusted to the light, she was surprised to see that the voice belonged to a woman.

'I'd like to see Doctor Goodman,' she said.

'He's busy.'

'I am Miss Hale, from Darkwater. I would like to talk to him about Mrs. Dere, if I may. When he has a moment, of course. I don't wish to intrude.'

The hand on the door paused. The woman said, after a moment, 'You may come in, but I don't know when he will be able to see you. He is busy.'

When she had come into the hall and blinked her eyes once or twice, Jennifer could see that the housekeeper (for that she surely was, her white apron and cap marked her as a servant) more clearly. She was middle-aged and when she walked it was with a strange, rocking tread that made the floorboards creak.

'Wait here,' she commanded, indicating a plain wooden chair that sat in the hallway. 'I will see if the doctor has time to see you.'

Her manner and tone made it plain that she resented having been forced to do so by virtue of Jennifer's use of the name Dere, and Darkwater. The housekeeper would not have dared to refuse her admittance, knowing that she came from there, but she did not like being challenged.

A very thin and obviously frightened maid suddenly appeared along the hall. She was hardly more than twelve or thirteen, without a curve to her spare body and she cringed in a habitual manner.

The housekeeper saw a fit object for her anger and she roared, 'Nelly where were you when the knocker was banging? What you want is a good whipping again and I'll see that you get it good, you hear?'

'Yes'm,' Nelly said, stepping aside and cowering, but her humble attitude and bent head did not prevent her receiving a resounding slap. The girl did not lift her eyes although she whimpered faintly.

Jennifer made note of the girl's pale complexion and her obvious fear, and she thought, if Walter sends Liza into servitude, that is what she will suffer. No, I cannot blame him for refusing to do that.

The housekeeper disappeared through a door. At once the frightened little maid scurried away and was gone from sight as well.

It was a shock to see such behavior and yet Jennifer knew it was not so unusual. So many girls had been driven into servitude since the war, and she was well aware that many of them were treated as badly as the unfortunate Nelly . . . and some of them far worse.

It might be that Liza, if she were sent out to work, would fare better. Beyond question there were many good families in the South, families who treated their servants with affection and gentleness, but there was always the other possibility too.

Liza was no meek lamb, either, like Nelly. Liza was proud and willful. What might Liza suffer if she found herself in confrontation with a cruel overseer?

The housekeeper returned, moving along the hall in her curiously heavy way. 'The doctor will see you,' she said, obviously unhappy to deliver the news. 'Come with me.'

Jennifer followed her. She found herself in a waiting room, painted a pristine white and as neat as a pin. Several chairs and a settee had been placed around the room and Jennifer seated herself in one of the chairs.

She hadn't long to wait. In a moment, an inner door opened and a man in a white smock appeared.

'Miss Hale?' he greeted her. 'I am Doctor Goodman. My housekeeper said you wanted to see me. Won't you come in, please?'

He led her into his examining room. Jennifer's first impression of the doctor was favorable. He looked kindly and rather old-fashioned. His thatch of white hair refused to be combed, but stuck out impertinently on all sides. Spectacles hung at a precarious angle on the top of his nose, and behind them his eyes twinkled with a jollity that belied his serious expression and scientific profession.

'Now then,' he said when Jennifer had seated herself in the chair he indicated, 'what seems to be the matter?'

'With me, nothing,' she said, smiling. 'I've come to you about Mrs. Dere. Mrs. Alicia Dere, that is. I understand she is a patient of yours.'

'Yes, that she is. And you are the new companion. We've heard of you here in town.' His twinkling eyes told her that she had been the object of much gossip and speculation since her arrival.

'I suppose newcomers are not so common here,' she said. 'And no doubt anything to do with the Deres is of utmost interest.'

'Exactly,' he said, bobbing his head to acknowledge that they did indeed understand one another. 'But, about Mrs. Dere . . . ?'

'I thought perhaps you could tell me a little about her condition.' She saw his frown and quickly added, 'I appreciate the doctor-patient relationship, of course.

But I am meant to be her nurse as well as her companion, and I need to know a little more about what is wrong with her.'

The doctor hesitated for a moment. Then, as if he had reached a decision, he said abruptly, 'Nothing.'

'I beg your pardon.'

'Nothing is wrong with Mrs. Dere,' he said, seating himself on the opposite side of his desk from her. 'That is to say, nothing medical. I have examined her again and again and I can find nothing at all wrong with the woman.'

'I rather thought as much myself. I had the impression she was malingering. And yet . . . '

He nodded his head in understanding. 'Yes, there is that 'and yet,' isn't there? There is no doubt that she feels poorly. She could not be pretending all of that.'

'Frankly, there have been times when I thought surely her physical pain must be real. She suffers so with it.'

'The mind is a powerful thing.'

'Yes, that is true.' Jennifer paused, thinking. 'Don't you think that some fresh air and sunshine, and maybe a little exercise . . . ?'

'They would do no harm, and probably some good. If you could get her to agree to them. But there is more to it than that, I'm sure of it. She is tragically unhappy, and I believe it is this that is making her ill.'

He looked for a moment as if he were going to venture his opinion as to the cause of this unhappiness, but at the last minute he thought better of it. She was, after all, only a paid servant of the Deres and he their physician, and they could hardly begin to gossip about the Dere's personal business.

Jennifer stood up. 'Then there is nothing you can advise me to do so far as the care of Mrs. Dere?'

'Try to keep her calm and avoid the sort of excitement that brings on her spells. And it might not be a bad idea to pursue your notion of getting her outside a little bit each day. But I wouldn't insist on it if she doesn't feel so inclined. Most of all, I think she wants babying. Perhaps if her husband spent a little time with her, it would cheer her up somewhat . . . ' He let his voice trail off. That was as far as he dared venture into that subject.

'I will do what I can.' She started for the door, but before she reached it, a thought occurred to her and she turned back.

'Doctor, do you know a woman who lives in the swamp, Mrs. Hodges?'

He smiled and nodded. 'Yes. The people hereabouts call her the swamp witch. I would avoid her if I were you. She's mostly harmless, but certainly unstable.'

'Do you think . . . ?' She hesitated. 'Do you believe she is a witch?'

He gave her a look of mild reproach. 'No, I don't believe that, but she has effected some cures that seemed like magic to folks hereabout. She's very knowledgeable about herbs and natural methods of healing, and there are miracles that can be worked with them if one knows enough. I wish I knew more. She has cured one or two cases where medical science was helpless. But that is not real magic, it is only advanced knowledge. That is all the Middle Ages witches were, you know, people who were misfits and who were, in many cases, ahead of their time in the knowledge they possessed, the same kind of knowledge, of herbs and berries and such. But why do you ask about Mrs. Hodges?'

'I was only curious. I had heard she was the mother of a girl living at Darkwater, Liza. Do you know the child?'

'Yes, but I could hardly believe she is Mrs. Hodges daughter. The woman is seventy if she's a day, and Liza can't be more than thirteen or fourteen.'

'She could be a granddaughter, perhaps.'

'It is possible,' he said with a shrug. 'But I would still doubt it very much. That would presuppose that at some time Mrs. Hodges had a child of her own, and if she did, no one around here ever heard of it. She has lived in this neighborhood for decades, you see, and surely someone would have known if she had a child. Word gets around.'

'I suppose that is so. But I'm told Mr. Dere found her with Mrs. Hodges. If she is not Mrs. Hodges daughter, where do you suppose she came from?'

Another shrug. 'There was so much confusion after the war. Children were abandoned by families who could not care for them. I suspect if the truth were known, and probably it never will be, that was the case with Liza. Someone — an unmarried woman, a derelict mother, a family whose fortunes had been destroyed — left her somewhere in the hope that someone would find her who could care for her. In this case, that someone was apparently Mrs. Hodges.'

The doctor was right, of course. Mrs. Hodges was much too old to be Liza's mother. If she herself had not been so shaken by her encounter with Mrs. Hodges, Jennifer would have realized this for herself at once. And Alicia, surely Alicia was intelligent enough to accept the truth for herself.

Most likely the truth was something along the lines of the scenario the doctor had outlined. But if Liza was not Mrs. Hodge's child, whose child was she, and how had she come to be living in the swamp with the old woman?

Helen had not yet returned to the trap. Jennifer went along to the Emporium and found Helen there, waiting while the clerk wrapped a bolt of fabric for her.

'The children need some new clothes. Liza is too big already for her clothes. They were mostly hand-me-downs anyway.'

Again Jennifer was struck with the treatment afforded Liza, as if she were one of the family and yet not quite that either. She knew Helen did not care for having Liza there, and resented her. At the same time, her sense of fairness and her natural affection for children made it impossible for her to be really cruel to the child.

Surely, Jennifer thought, Liza must instinctively sense this ambivalence of feeling toward her. No doubt that was part of the explanation for her aloofness.

By the time they had finished their shopping and had made the drive back to Darkwater it was later afternoon. The return trip was pleasant. Helen kept to herself any curiosity she might have felt regarding Jennifer's visit to Doctor Goodman.

Perhaps, Jennifer thought, that was because she too had concluded there was nothing physically wrong with Alicia, and that her spells sprang from unhappiness and her possessively jealous nature.

For that ailment, Jennifer saw no relief. She felt certain herself that sending Liza away would not solve the problem. With Liza gone, Alicia would only look around for someone else toward whom to direct her jealousy and resentment. And Jennifer did not have to look far to guess who that would be.

'By the way,' Helen said as they came up the drive to Darkwater, 'we will be having company this evening for dinner.'

Since Jennifer had been at Darkwater there were frequently guests at dinner, but this, she gathered, was something a bit different.

'Is there an occasion?'

'Some of the local men are talking of forming a grange. They want to discuss it with Walter after dinner. Of course they'll be bringing their families with them.'

'Perhaps I can help by looking after the children.'

'There will be servants enough for that. And some of the children are old enough to help look after the others. You will be more of an asset at the dinner table, and perhaps afterward, in the parlor. Do you play the pianoforte?'

'A little. But I'm not an artist, I'm afraid.'

Helen dismissed that with a wave of her hand. 'Folks out here get hungry for entertainment. If you can manage to bang out a tune on the keys, they won't be too critical, I assure you.'

Jennifer hesitated a moment before asking, 'Will Alicia be with us for dinner?'

'She rarely feels well enough for company,' Helen said, her voice dry and noncommittal. 'I rather expect she will have a tray in her room, as she usually does.'

Later, in her own room, it occurred to Jennifer that she had been virtually asked to help act as hostess in Alicia's place. It gave her a thrill to think of acting as Walter's hostess, greeting his friends and entertaining them.

She knew she should feel guilt for her happiness, but she could not. Helen could not suspect how she felt about Walter. It was the sort of favor she would have asked of any female living in the house, but to her, it was like every wonderful happening rolled into one. For this night, at least, she could pretend, pretend that she and Walter were not doomed to be forever apart, that he did not have a wife already, and that there might be some prospect of happiness for them.

She wore her best dress that evening, the gray silk Worth, and although it was clearly well worn, she knew it made a good impression upon the ladies when she entered the dining room.

She did not pay so much attention to what the men thought, except one. She glanced in Walter's direction and found his eyes on her. Was it only her imagination or was there a gleam of appreciation in them? Surely he rose to his feet more quickly than the others, and moved to hold her chair for her.

In addition to herself and Helen and

Walter, and Susan and Martin Donally, there were three other couples, the Mortons, the Sands, and the Baumgardners.

That these last two couples should even be at this dinner party said something about the new South that had emerged from the ashes of the war. The Sands, she knew at once, were creoles, descendants from the original French settlers of Louisiana. Of dark complexions and dark hair, the creoles had in the past looked with disdain upon the 'Merican coquin, those flatboatmen and swindlers from the North, as they saw it, who had dared to try to mingle with the aristocratic creoles.

The Baumgardners were of that breed of German settlers who had come to this rich new land and had, many of them, carved out vast estates for themselves. He was a man of about fifty, fat and florid but with a sort of robust vitality that made him seem younger and slimmer. His wife was pale and puffy, a soft little creature without angles or lines, only lush curves. She spoke with the thick accent he had almost lost.

The Mortons were young, in their thirties and energetic. It was such as these, Jennifer believed, who would rebuild the South. The old aristocracy had gone soft, spoiled by luxury. The Deres had fared well partly because they were strong, hard-working people. Even Helen, obviously bred to wealth and class, could put herself to work in the kitchen without any seeming distaste for menial tasks.

For this occasion, Darkwater did itself proud. From somewhere Bess had produced extra servants to help prepare and serve the food. The dining room looked lovely. Although it was not furnished in what could be considered a luxuriant manner, the pieces there were good and old and handsome, and tonight they were at their best advantage, polished until one could see one's face in the gleaming wood. Arrangements of flowers had been placed about the room and scores of candles flickered softly, and the mismatched dishes that the family used from day to day had been replaced with what was surely 'the good china.'

It had been many years since Jennifer had been seated at a meal like this. Because day to day life at Darkwater was simple, it was easy to forget that the Deres were aristocrats and, by the standards of the time, wealthy.

On this night, she was reminded as course followed course, each more beautiful and tastier than the one before. Bess had made use of the local food available, whereas in the past delicacies of every imaginable sort might have been imported for the occasion — but Louisiana could provide a table in abundance, as the dinner proved. From the swamps came frog's legs and crayfish and shrimp, and from the forests, game birds and a wild pig. From right here on Darkwater came chicken for the *poulet noir*, and the greens and the sugar with which the yams were sweetened.

Jennifer felt as if she were intoxicated, although she barely sipped at the wine set before her. She thought of her mother, and of the years of deprivation, and a wave of sadness made her eyes smart. The food at this table would have fed them for months.

'I had thought you would enjoy the diversion,' Walter said at one point, leaning close to her, 'but you look as if it makes you want to cry.'

'Perhaps it does,' she said, but she beamed because he had noticed her and had taken the trouble to try to cheer her.

Alicia did not appear at the table. As Helen had predicted, she remained in her room, ostensibly eating from a tray. She did manage to make her presence felt, however. As the group was sitting down to dinner, Alicia rang the bell in her room and demanded to see her husband. Dinner waited while he answered the summons. Jennifer could not know what transpired between husband and wife, but when Walter returned after several minutes, his face was flushed with anger.

Later, as dinner progressed, he was twice more called away and Jennifer could see that his patience was being sorely strained. She herself could not understand why Alicia had chosen not to join the guests. She herself had tried to persuade Alicia that she was quite well enough to eat at the table with them, but Alicia had remained convinced otherwise.

'What do you know of the way I feel?' Alicia had demanded petulantly. 'I lie here suffering and no one knows or even cares.'

Well then, Jennifer had thought, dropping the subject, let her sit alone and miss everything if she chooses.

Despite Alicia's interruptions, the dinner went well. There was some brief conversation among the men regarding the prospective grange, but that was generally deferred until the ladies had withdrawn.

Jennifer understood a little about the organization. It was generally regarded as the country's first important farmers' movement, and it had begun in the Midwest, where farmers there had begun to form organizations they called Patrons of Husbandry, which became commonly known as granges. They were organized to combat the unfair practices of railways and grain elevators, and they had been successful in having protective legislation passed, legislation that touched deeply upon the subject of states' rights. As a result, granges had begun to spring up about the country, even in the Deep South where farming before had been an independent and gentlemanly pursuit.

She saw the looks of surprise from the men when she joined in their conversations on the subject and indeed she would have been glad to pursue it but the men did not think that suitable.

'We don't want to bore the ladies with such serious talk,' Mr. Morton said and the others nodded agreement and began to discuss the opera in New Orleans before the war.

Jennifer and Helen exchanged a quick glance. In some ways it was still very much the Old South, Jennifer thought. Women were meant to be pretty playthings, with little practical value.

When dinner was finished, the women retired to the withdrawing room while the men lingered over their port and passed around cigars.

For herself, Jennifer would as soon have lingered with the men. Although she suspected all the women present were intelligent and thoughtful, she was dismayed to see that their conversation was limited to 'women talk.' They discussed their homes, their husbands, their children. They would not be persuaded by Jennifer to discuss literature nor the state of the South since the war, nor anything else of consequence.

Jennifer escaped once to look in on the children. With those who had come with the visiting couples, plus the Dere children and Liza, there were an even dozen. A table had been set up for them in one of the spare rooms, where they had eaten. By this time their meal was over too and the table had been cleared so they could play games.

When Jennifer came into the room, Liza was holding court. She was only slightly older than some of the others, but the impression she gave was that she was minding them all and doing so by keeping them entertained. At the moment she was engaged in telling them some story, the import of which Jennifer did not get.

' . . . By a witch,' was all she heard as

she came in, but at the sound of the door opening, Liza's narration stopped and everyone turned in Jennifer's direction.

'I was only looking in to see that everything was all right,' Jennifer said, aware that her presence was a distraction. 'Do go on, please.'

She left, and not until the door had closed and she was walking away did she hear the murmur of Liza's voice begin again.

By this time the men had finished their port and the entire party was now assembled in the parlor. When Jennifer came in, someone said, 'Here she is now.'

Helen said, 'I promised them you would play some music for us.'

Embarrassed, Jennifer said, 'But I am really not very accomplished.'

'I would certainly enjoy to hear some music,' a voice close to her said. She looked up into Walter's eyes and knew she could not refuse after that request.

'Very well,' she said, taking a seat at the pianoforte. 'I will play, but only if everyone sings.'

She brought her hands down upon the keys, hesitantly at first and then with more confidence, and began to play a spirited rendition of 'Camptown Races.' Shyly at first and then with gusto, those who gathered about the piano began to sing. By the time she was playing the second chorus, everyone was singing loudly and happily, making the walls ring with their voices.

She kept them singing with 'Nellie Gray.' And then she grew more serious, beginning to play an Irish song she had heard during the war, 'The Rose of Tralee.' Until then she had not sung but now, as the others did not know the song, she began to sing it for them, her sweet girlish soprano only a whisper as she began, then soaring until it filled the room with the song's haunting melody and the tender lyrics.

When she finished, she was surprised by the brief hush that lingered after the last chord. Then, in unison, her listeners began to applaud. She flushed with embarrassment.

'That was lovely,' one of the women

said, and another said, 'It filled my eyes with tears.'

Jennifer looked around and saw that Walter, who had stepped back a pace or two, was beaming at her with pride. His smile thanked her more than the spoken words of the others.

She played 'Annie Laurie' next, insisting that they all sing with her, and then, so that the party not become too maudlin, she finished with 'Captain Jinks.'

By the time she rose from the instrument the mood of fun and gaiety had been restored. There were loud protests that she should stop playing.

'My hands are not accustomed to the effort,' she said. 'I am afraid I am too tired to continue to play.'

She again excused herself, thinking that she would look in on the children. This time when she opened the door to the room they were in, they paid less attention to her. They did not even seem to notice her, in fact, so absorbed were they in what Liza was doing.

She was at one end of the table with

the others clustered in front of her, their eyes glued to her hands. She held what looked to be a crude doll, fashioned, so far as Jennifer could see from the doorway, of feathers and straw, and apparently intended to represent a chicken. Liza moved it back and forth, jiggling it to give a remarkably effective impression of a hen waddling.

'Cluck, cluck,' Liza said. She held her 'hen' up, so that everyone could see it clearly. Then she put it on the table and began to wave her hands over it as if performing some magic ceremony.

'What . . . ?' Jennifer started to ask, but someone shushed her so firmly that she held her tongue and watched, as mesmerized now by Liza's mysterious actions as the children were.

'Cluck, cluck' Liza said again and, seizing the straw hen, she lifted it from the table. There, immediately beneath where it had lain, was a fresh egg. The children applauded this sleight-of-hand and Jennifer impulsively joined in, wondering how on earth Liza had managed to pull off the stunt.

'Do it again,' one of the children cried.

'Yes, do it again,' Came a chorus of voices.

Liza looked toward the door and Jennifer. She had been so engrossed in her trick that she had not even noticed Jennifer come into the room until she lifted the hen to show the egg. Seeing Jennifer, she looked doubtful and even, Jennifer thought, a little frightened.

No wonder Alicia thinks she is a witch, Jennifer thought, if Liza can perform her little tricks so neatly. Aloud, she said, with an encouraging smile, 'Yes, please do it again. I should like to see it.'

The performance with the image of straw and chicken feathers was repeated. Jennifer observed that Liza, like all good performers, kept her audience's attention where she wanted it. So effective were her hand movements that Jennifer forgot to watch to see how she slipped the egg into place until it was too late.

Once again the hen was lifted to reveal a shining white egg on the tabletop. The sight was greeted with a chorus of giggles and cheers from the children. It was this unfortunate moment, however, that Alicia had chosen to appear in the doorway, and her reaction to the stunt was far less appreciative.

'There!' she cried from behind Jennifer, who had not even been aware of her approach. 'Didn't I tell you she was a witch? That proves it.'

'Alicia, I . . . ' Jennifer tried to take hold of her, to calm her down, but Alicia was beside herself. She rushed into the room and seized the egg from the table.

'You see, it's still warm, just as if it had come from a real chicken.' She turned on Liza and before Jennifer could stop her, she had struck the child across the face.

'Witch!' she screamed at the top of her voice. 'Witch, witch, witch!'

6

Throughout the evening Alicia had sulked in her room. What right had they to have a party when she was too ill to attend? It showed gross indifference to the state of her health. For all they cared, she could die here while they had their party.

And that simpering companion, Jennifer. 'If you feel you are being left out, why don't you get out of bed and join us for dinner? I'm sure everyone would be delighted and I'll be glad to help you all I can.'

As if there were nothing at all wrong with her, as if she were just making it all up. She knew that was what they believed, all of them, probably even that stupid doctor. What did they know of what she suffered every day? If they knew, or cared at all, Walter would have done what she asked long ago and gotten rid of that awful witch-child.

They were fools, all of them, taken in

by that put-on air of innocence. That child of the swamp. And while they simpered and prattled and had their dinner parties, she, Alicia, was dying.

She caught at her throat, tugging at the ribbon she wore there. If felt as if it were choking her. With a gesture of impatience she yanked it free and threw it on the floor, but the feeling lingered, as if ghostly hands were squeezing at her throat.

'It's that girl and her tricks,' she muttered. From the parlor came the sound of singing. She listened to a girlish voice. It must be Jennifer, it certainly could not be Helen, singing a song she did not know. It had a poignant, lingering melody and suddenly her eyes filled with tears.

She felt so alone, so unloved and unwanted. She thought of Walter and nearly reached for the bell to ring for him, but at the last moment she stayed her hand. He would come along when she rang, sit and hold her hand, his face wooden and his voice unfeeling, and assure her that everything was all right.

Annie Laurie. Now they were singing Annie Laurie, and even at the distance she could pick out Walter's rich baritone and Jennifer's sweet soprano.

Those two, always exchanging glances. As if she weren't supposed to see, as if she were too stupid to figure them out. She had seen Walter's eyes devouring Jennifer's slim young figure, had seen lust in his eyes — naked, ugly animal lust. He never came to his own wife's bed, but he could lust after any pretty young woman who came around.

Well, let him lust, Alicia thought, smiling bitterly to herself. So far it hadn't done him any good, she was sure of that.

Would they never finish with that blasted song? 'Gave me her promise true . . . which ne'er forgot will be . . . ' She mouthed the words, her voice a hoarse croaking whisper.

Of course, if Jennifer ever encouraged him . . . but she wouldn't, not her. And it suited Alicia to have her around. At least she was someone who listened to her, who gave her a little bit of attention. Besides, she was keeping her eye on that Liza. Jennifer had promised she would do that.

If only she could catch Liza up to her shenanigans. Then they would all know she was right, and that she wasn't crazy. Then Walter would have to get rid of the brat.

Hardly even thinking about what she meant to do, she got out of the bed and grabbed the robe that was always close at hand. She would discover for herself what mischief Liza was up to.

She was not even aware that the singing had finished some minutes before. She stole along the hall, knowing where she would find the children.

As she came near, she heard the sound of childish laughter and applause. She paused for a minute or so, wondering what the children were doing. Perhaps she should wait until Liza was alone.

Curiosity prodded her to go on, however, and she went to the open door. She was surprised to see Jennifer in the room, her back to the hall, and the children were all gathered around the table, watching something.

Noiselessly Alicia moved into the room, so that she could see past Jennifer's shoulder. She saw Liza holding something in her hand, moving it around. When she set it down, Alicia saw that it was a kind of doll, done up to look like a hen.

What on earth, she wondered, frowning? The child began to wave her hands over the doll and Alicia felt a cold chill, and then a glimmer of triumph. Perhaps this was it, the opportunity she had been waiting for, to catch that evil child in one of her witch acts.

Liza lifted the doll — and there on the table was an egg. It had not been there before, Alicia was certain of that. It had been laid, by a handful of straw and feathers. And if that wasn't witchcraft, she surely didn't know what was.

That was when she screamed.

* * *

It was unfortunate that the incident had to occur with so many people in the house, Jennifer was to think later. If they had been alone — but then, Liza would probably not have been performing her little stunt.

As it was, Alicia's screams brought everyone from the parlor, crowding into the room with the children. Jennifer tried to assure them it was only a trick, but Alicia was hysterical and had to be carried back to bed. By that time, Liza was so frightened she could not do her trick again, to show the others how harmless it was.

'Well, show us how you did it, anyway,' Helen demanded.

Jennifer saw that Liza was on the verge of tears, and she interceded. 'Please,' she said, 'I think Liza needs to go to bed.'

Despite disappointment, the others had to agree that she was right, and Jennifer managed to spirit Liza away from the crowd and up to her room.

Liza was even more than usually subdued, but she allowed Jennifer to help her undress and get ready for bed. For perhaps they first time since they had met, she did not seem to be at odds with Jennifer.

When she was almost ready for bed,

Liza said, 'Do you think Walter will be angry with me?'

'I think it is safe to say you caused a bit of an uproar,' Jennifer said. 'Alicia will not get over this too quickly.'

Liza shot her a startled look. 'What will she do?'

'Why, I . . . I don't know,' Jennifer said, seeing genuine fear in the girl's eyes. 'Now I don't think you need to worry unduly about that. Alicia is a little hysterical but at heart she's probably very fair. And Walter certainly will not let anything too terrible happen.'

'She'll make him send me away. Oh, don't let them do that.' She suddenly threw herself against Jennifer and flung her arms about her, clinging wildly.

For a moment Jennifer had the odd feeling that Liza was only play-acting. She saw that Liza's tears were genuine, however, and the feeling passed. She patted her shoulder comfortingly. 'There, now, there's nothing to be gained by getting yourself worked up over this.'

'But promise me, you won't let them send me away.'

'Why, it's not up to me, I'm sure. I only work here, don't you remember?'

'But they listen to you. Alicia listens to you, and Walter likes you, so he'll listen. He'll do whatever you tell him to do.'

Jennifer stiffened and although they were alone in the room, she felt her face turn red. Liza didn't know what she was saying, of course, she did not mean it to sound the way it did.

'I think you had better get into bed now,' she said firmly.

But when Liza was in bed and Jennifer on her way out, she said, 'You will talk to them, won't you?'

'Yes, I will talk to them.'

★ ★ ★

Alicia's hysterical outburst had effectively ended the party. Amid the flurry of leave-taking, Jennifer could not help but observe the scarcely contained excitement of the ladies. By midday tomorrow, no doubt most of the countryside would know of Alicia's latest outburst, with vivid details, perhaps some of them invented.

She joined the Deres while they bade their guests goodnight. When the door had closed on the last of them, Jennifer went alone to the parlor. She felt the need of a few moments to compose her thoughts.

Liza had observed something between her and Walter, something that transcended physical contact. Even if she did not really know what she was saying, Liza's remark must indicate that she had seen, or instinctively guessed, the threatening closeness between them.

There was only one thing she could do. She must leave Darkwater, before others reached the same conclusion. What if Alicia should discern how she felt? Or even Helen. It would be scandal. More, it would mean pain for Walter and his family, pain she had no right to inflict. No, she must go away. Even in her short time here, she had accumulated some money, enough to take her away, at least. She had found this position, surely she could find another. She would tell Walter at once.

She jumped to her feet and went in

search of Walter, determined to resolve things while she still had the will to act.

Walter and Helen were not in the hall near the door, where she had left them. She wondered if perhaps they had gone up to bed. But, no, they would not do that without putting out the lamps.

She heard their voices coming from the dining room. Not until she was at the door did she realize they were quarreling. Her first instinct was to leave, but before she could do so, she could not help overhearing a part of their argument.

'That child must leave,' Helen was saying in a firm voice. 'If there is to be any peace in this house ever again, you must send her out to work.'

'I can't,' Walter said. 'You know what that means for a young girl. I won't do it.'

'You must. It is the only way.'

'I gave her my word I would see she was taken care of.'

Jennifer did not hear the rest because she was already walking away. She did not wish to be guilty of eavesdropping. At the same time, though, she had promised Liza she would speak to the Deres on her behalf. She hesitated, wondering if perhaps this would not be the best opportunity to do so.

Instead, she returned to the parlor. She did not know what she should do. She could admit that there was some validity to what Helen had said. There was no doubt that Liza was a part of the discord that reigned here at Darkwater, seething just below the surface and sometimes erupting as it did tonight.

But was sending her away the answer? Or is the answer to go myself, Jennifer wondered?

She went to the piano, her fingers idly running over the keys, softly picking out the melody to 'The Last Rose of Summer.'

'That's a very sad song,' Walter said from behind her.

'Perhaps not so much sad as reflective,' she said, turning toward him. 'I did not hear you coming.'

'Maybe I wanted it that way. Maybe I wanted a moment to look at you without your running away from me.'

She felt her face turn crimson but she did not avoid his eyes. 'I heard part of your conversation just now. I did not mean to eavesdrop. I was looking for you to tell you something.'

'Then you know that Helen wants me to send Liza away?'

She nodded. Her heart was pounding and she knew she should have told him without hesitation what it was she had intended to tell him.

He sighed, totally absorbed now in his continuing problem with Liza. 'I don't know what to do. Alicia believes that Liza is responsible for her illness. It's nonsense, of course, but Alicia believes it and that amounts to the same thing in the long run.'

He shook his head and began to pace back and forth. 'But, to send her way . . . I promised her a home here. It seems so heartless to turn her out now. You know what it's like for a girl in service.'

'I know that it can certainly be dreadful.' She started to say something more and hesitated. She did not want to overstep the boundaries of their relationship — and yet, perhaps if she knew more, she could help more.

'Tell me about Liza,' she said impulsively. 'How did you happen to bring her here?'

He looked at her oddly and she thought briefly that he resented her question, but he did not say so.

'I found her in the swamp.' He spoke slowly at first, as if he held back from telling this story, but gradually the words came more freely and he sounded relieved to be sharing it with her.

'I was out hunting and I heard someone cry out. I thought someone had gotten hurt, as can happen in the swamp, and I followed the sounds. What I found was old Mrs. Hodges, beating a young girl with a stick.'

'Of course I made her stop and demanded an explanation. She told me Liza was her daughter. I knew that wasn't true, but she stuck to her story. Liza couldn't stop crying long enough to tell me anything, and she was obviously still terrified of Mrs. Hodges. If you could have seen how the little girl cowered, and clung to me when she thought I was going to leave her there.' He gave his head a shake, remembering.

'Finally I took Liza away with me. Mrs. Hodges ran after me for a time, cursing me and threatening me with all kinds of dire calamities — I suppose you know, the local folks believe she is a witch.'

'So I have heard.'

'Finally I warned her that I would use my influence to have her sent away from here altogether. That had some effect, and she left us, still muttering and shaking her fist.

'Once she had gone, I was able to get Liza calmed down enough to talk to me. She told me her parents had been part of a traveling carnival, and they had both died in an accident. Her father's partner took over the show and for a time she had lived with him, but he was cruel to her, in unspeakable ways, and she ran away, into the swamp. But she got lost and wandered for days before Mrs. Hodges found her. By then she was so tired and hungry that she couldn't go any further, and she stayed with Mrs. Hodges in that shack of hers.'

He paused for a moment and resumed

his pacing, back and forth. She did not intrude on his thoughts with questions, sure that he would finish his story in his own time.

'Eventually, Mrs. Hodges came to think of Liza as her own daughter, don't ask me why. But she also began to make demands on her. She made her work until she was exhausted, and if Liza did not do just as she was told, Mrs. Hodges would beat her until the child begged for mercy. It was on one of those occasions that I happened along and brought Liza back here with me.'

He turned and looked directly into Jennifer's eyes. 'I promised her a home. How can I turn around now and send her away again to the same sort of treatment or maybe even worse?'

Her heart went out to this big, rugged man who could at the same time express such concern for another's well-being.'

'I don't believe you can,' she said softly.

'But, Alicia . . . '

' . . . Is Alicia. She is jealous by nature, and possessive, and she is consumed with her own discontent. I believe that if you were to send Liza away, things would be a little better for a short while, until Alicia found another target for her bitterness. Forgive me, I have no right to speak like this of your wife . . . '

'No, it's all right. I want you to speak freely. What of Alicia's illness?'

'The doctor says there is nothing wrong with her medically. I do not know what you can do, but it has been my own observation that to give in to such a condition is to encourage it to worsen. Thus far everyone has gone along with the idea of Alicia's dire illness. Perhaps if you were firm . . . it might help. I don't know. I'm not a doctor, of course.'

'No,' he said in a voice so soft it could barely be heard. 'Only an angel. Only the best thing that ever came into my life.'

She knew that now was the time to speak, to tell him of her decision to leave Darkwater, but for a moment the words would not come, and then it was too late.

'Promise me you won't leave,' he said, as if he had read her thoughts. 'Stay here and help us. We need you here. I need you. And Alicia needs you too, of course.

It has helped her already, having someone like you in the house.'

'How can you say that, after tonight?'

'These outbursts are not new, I can assure you of that. She had as many or more before. At least you have made things a little more pleasant for . . . for all of us.'

She knew of course that she could not go now, not after he had asked her to stay, not after he had told her he needed her. Though the darkest tragedy might threaten, though she might forfeit every chance for happiness in the future, she knew she would remain, close at his side, to serve in any way that he might need her. To do otherwise would be to betray herself, to betray her innermost desires.

She had not spoken in a long moment. Anxiously he said: 'You will stay, won't you?'

He leaned toward her, as if he meant to kiss her, and her heart went pounding — but Helen appeared at the door just then. She stopped, saying nothing, only looking from one to the other.

'Good night,' Jennifer said, and before

either could say anything further, she was by them and out of the room, running toward the stairs.

★ ★ ★

It was doubly unfortunate that the following day Mrs. Baumgardner added to the story of Liza's 'witchcraft' with the news that her prize laying hen had died mysteriously during the night. By midday the story had spread through the environs of Durieville and returned to Darkwater with the servants.

Bess heard the story from a friend, and after pooh-poohing it firmly, she came to tell Helen, who also pooh-poohed it, but could not help worrying about the consequences of such gossip circulating.

'If Walter tries to send Liza into service after this, it will be doubly hard,' she said in relating the story to Jennifer.

Jennifer already knew that Walter did not intend to send Liza into service, but she could not help thinking that this gave Walter an excuse to follow his own intentions. With a wile born of her love for him, she seized the first opportunity to point this out to Alicia.

'You have only yourself to blame if Liza is still in the house,' she said when, later that same day, Alicia asked if Walter had made any plans to send her away. 'If you will insist upon screaming to the entire neighborhood that the girl is a witch, you can hardly wonder if people are afraid of her.'

'But you do believe she is a witch, don't you?' Alicia asked. 'You saw what she was doing with that effigy.'

'I saw her doing sleight-of-hand, just like tricksters do at carnivals. And as she says her parents were carnival people, it is hardly surprising that she learned a few of their tricks.'

Alicia sulked. 'No one cares if she is killing me with her black magic tricks.' But it was clear that Jennifer's remark had hit home, because she soon dropped the subject of Liza's witchery.

The result was that things were very peaceful again at Darkwater during the next few days. After a week or so, even the gossip died down, and while no one wanted to forget the stories about Liza's witchcraft and Alicia's hysteria, they soon lost their relish.

Jennifer did what she could to maintain the peace. She discovered the next day that Liza felt grateful for her intervention and she quickly took advantage of that fact. She did not mind playing upon other people's feelings in this instance, knowing that what she did was for Walter as well as for the general good.

'If you are really grateful,' she told Liza, 'you will keep the promise I made.'

'What's that?' Liza asked, the old suspicion creeping into her voice.

'You will do what you can to keep the peace in the house. And that means, no upsetting Alicia.'

Liza looked sullen. 'Alicia gets upset over nothing.'

'Then the thing for you to do,' Jennifer said, not to be put off so easily, 'is to avoid her. Stay out of her room. Play somewhere where she cannot see or hear you. Let her forget you're here.'

'I hate her,' Liza said vehemently.

'It's wrong to hate.'

'Do you think it's wrong for me to hate her but it's all right for her to hate me?'

'I don't think it's ever right to hate. But in order to stop it, one person has to stop first.'

Despite Liza's resistance, Jennifer observed that during the next few days she was scrupulous in avoiding Alicia's company and in doing nothing to irritate her. It began to look as if some sort of domestic tranquility had at last arrived at Darkwater. The others, too, remarked on this.

'I can't get over how quiet it's been around here,' Helen said one day.

Susan, who was there for lunch, said, 'Maybe after her last outburst, Alicia has let off some steam.'

Only Walter was suspicious of the new quiet. Perhaps, Jennifer thought, noticing the uneasy glances he cast toward Alicia's door, he has been too long living with that tension to give it up easily now.

Of all those involved, Alicia seemed to make the most effort to avoid further conflict. Indeed, since that unfortunate incident with the children, Alicia seemed to be experiencing something of a recovery. Only a few days later, she announced, with a note of surprise in her voice, that she was feeling better.

'I can hardly believe it,' she said, 'the pressure at my throat has lessened. I can actually breathe again without pain.'

Seeing an opportunity she had been looking for, Jennifer said, 'I wonder, then, if the time hasn't come to let nature do some of her work. Don't you think a little fresh air and sunshine would do you good?'

At first Alicia looked a little shocked at the suggestion, and then intrigued by the idea. Almost shyly, she said, 'I haven't been outside in over a year.'

'Then I think you are overdue,' Jennifer said decisively, smiling. She was still convinced that if only she could get Alicia interested in recovering, get her to mentally 'let go' of her suffering, she would be on the road to total recovery. And a return to the simple delight of sitting outside on a lovely summer day was surely a step in the right direction.

The very next day found them making the trip from Alicia's room to the front yard. It seemed a long journey, and Alicia clung to Jennifer as they reached the front door, but it did not seem so much a matter of weakness, Jennifer thought, but of fear.

'My, I had forgotten how bright the Lusianna sun can be,' Alicia said, blinking from the shelter of the front porch, but she looked delighted to be there.

'I thought we would sit in the shade of that big oak,' Jennifer said, pointing. It was a vast old tree, with moss dripping from its gnarled branches. It cast a great shadow upon the lawn.

'That's the Dere oak,' Alicia said as they moved slowly toward it. 'According to the story, it was planted by the first Dere to settle here, and as long as it stands, the Deres will continue to reside here. There's more to it than that, oh, I don't know, Walter could tell you.'

The thought of the Dere family going on and on through generations gave Jennifer an odd pang. She would not be part of it. She would live out her life and die, and never know a husband, because the one man she would have for a husband was married to the woman clinging to her arm. It seemed suddenly as if the sun had dimmed.

'Isn't this nice, now?' Alicia said when they reached the spot under the tree. Earlier, Jennifer had directed the men to place a settee in the shade there, on which Alicia could recline, and a chair for Jennifer. A tray bearing glasses and Bess's fresh lemonade sat on a small table.

'I believe I will do this every day,' Alicia said, smiling about at her surroundings.

For the next several days, Alicia was as good as her word. With each day the results were dramatically obvious. Alicia's cheeks began to glow and her eyes took on a sparkle Jennifer had never seen in them before. Each day they lingered a little longer, and there was no doubt that the fresh air under the oak tree was exhilarating and reviving her.

'It's better than any medicine I can prescribe,' Doctor Goodman said when he came next to examine Alicia. 'Miss Hale, I congratulate you, you have done wonders with my patient.'

'Yes, it is all thanks to Jennifer,' Alicia

was quick to agree.

'It was a good day for us when you decided to come for the job,' Helen said, and Bess nodded her head in agreement. Walter stood at a distance and watched.

Later, looking back, Jennifer was to realize these were the last truly peaceful days at Darkwater. They were a moment of respite in the storm that was even then threatening to break about them.

It was to be expected that something would happen to end the quiet, and that when it did, it was between Liza and Alicia.

With Alicia up and moving about much more than before, it was inevitable that the two would meet, no matter how much everyone tried to keep them apart, but how they met was most unfortunate.

Alicia had been doing so well in getting around that she ventured one day to leave her room on her own. She had intended it for a surprise.

Won't Walter be surprised to see me at the table, she told herself, leaving her bedroom and starting slowly along the hall. It was time for dinner and she could hear the murmur of voices from the dining room. Earlier, she had told Jennifer she was not hungry yet and would like her tray a little later than usual.

She went slowly, supporting herself with a hand against the wall. She had nearly reached the dining room when a flurry of sound made her start. The next moment, Liza burst into the hall and collided with Alicia. The two of them went sprawling, taking a hall table with them.

'What on earth . . . ?' Helen appeared in the doorway, and Walter behind her a moment later.

Alicia burst into tears at being discovered in such an undignified position, sprawled on the floor like an unruly child, Liza lying half across her.

'Oh, you awful child,' Alicia cried, slapping angrily at Liza. 'You did that on purpose. I was trying to surprise Walter, to show him how good I was doing, and you've spoiled it, and you did it on purpose.'

'Alicia, be reasonable,' Walter said,

coming to help her up. 'How could Liza have known what you were planning? I certainly didn't. And she might have hurt herself as well in a spill like that.'

'That's right, take her part,' Alicia sobbed, slapping his hands away. 'That's all you can think of, that she might have been hurt. What about me? I wish she had been hurt. I wish she had broken her evil little neck.'

Liza said nothing. She sat woodenly on the floor, staring at Alicia as Jennifer helped Alicia to her feet.

'Come along, we'll help you into the dining room,' Jennifer said.

'No,' Alicia cried, 'I won't go there. I want to go back to my own room, where I belong and where that witch can't torment me.'

She would not let herself be persuaded otherwise. Jennifer gave in and helped her back to her bedroom. Once there, Alicia wanted to be helped into bed and, as she seemed even weaker than before, it was several minutes before Jennifer could excuse herself and return to the dining room.

'You all think I'm crazy,' Alicia said, 'but if I am, it's because she has driven me crazy, tormenting me with her tricks. You won't be happy until she's killed me.'

'Alicia, if anything is going to kill you it will be your own insistence that you are ill,' Jennifer said. She left before Alicia had time to reply.

'I do think . . . ' Jennifer began as she came into the dining room where the others waited, but Walter had anticipated her remark.

'I've already scolded Liza,' he said quietly. 'It was an unfortunate accident, and she shouldn't have been running in the house, but it was an accident. We all know that Alicia lets things get all out of proportion.'

Jennifer did not care to argue this further but she had certain reservations of her own. She had happened to glance down as she was helping Alicia to her feet, and she had seen the look Liza gave Alicia. It was a look of such venom that for a moment Jennifer had almost been willing to believe that Alicia was right and that Liza had caused the accident deliberately.

But how could she have known that Alicia was coming down the hall just then? Anyway, Liza was only a child, and it was the sort of accident any child might cause.

Still, she could not entirely rid herself of the odd feeling that perhaps there was some grain of truth to Alicia's insistence that Liza had deliberately caused the accident.

Anyway, Alicia had invited it. Perhaps, she thought, the two of them have fought so long now that fighting is a familiar comfort and without it they do not quite feel right.

In that case, she told herself, they should both be happy now, because undoubtedly the peace is broken.

As it turned out, she was more right even than she thought.

7

No one was surprised when Alicia had one of her 'spells' later that evening. What was surprising, at least to Jennifer, was the intensity of the attack. For the first time she began to take seriously the possibility that there might be something really wrong physically with Alicia.

'I can't breathe,' Alicia gasped, writhing upon her bed and clawing at her throat. 'I tell you, it's like someone is strangling me.'

Jennifer had gotten up from bed when Alicia's bell rang during the night. Walter had come down too but she sent him away, saying she would spend the night with Alicia. At first she thought it was just another of Alicia's emotional traumas and that when she had talked for a while, spilling out some of her venomous hatred for the child living in the house, she would fall asleep and Jennifer could return to the comfort of her bed.

Now she was not so sure. 'Tell me how you feel,' she said, leaning close over the bed. There was no doubt that the pain twisting Alicia's face into a grotesque mask was real. Jennifer wondered if she should send someone for Doctor Goodman.

'I can't breathe, I told you,' Alicia snapped. 'And I feel so weak, as if the life were being drained out of me. It's that girl, I tell you, that little witch.'

'Nonsense. You can't possibly believe that Liza could have anything to do with this. She's in her own bed by now, sound asleep.'

'Are you so sure? Have you looked?'

'Why, no,' Jennifer said, surprised. 'But what has that to do with it anyway? How can you think that she, wherever she is, could make it difficult for you to breathe?'

'The same way she made that handful of feathers and straw lay an egg. You saw her do that the same as I did. It was magic, black magic that she learned from her mother in that swamp. And she's killing me with it, and no one cares.'

With that Alicia burst into sobs,

flinging herself back against her pillow, but almost at once the sobs were cut off and she began to gasp and choke so violently that Jennifer was alarmed.

'Here, let me help you sit up,' she said, tugging at Alicia's shoulders. 'You'll breathe more easily sitting up.'

Together they got Alicia to a sitting position, the pillows propped up behind her, but even this did not seem to help much. By now Alicia was actually white with the effort of breathing and her eyes were wide with fright.

'I am going to send for the doctor,' Jennifer said.

'Don't . . . leave me,' Alicia whispered hoarsely. 'I . . . I'm so frightened . . . '

'I will only be gone a minute.' Jennifer went without waiting for further protest, and ran along the hall and up the stairs. Without even knocking, she opened the door to Helen's room and went in.

Helen sat up in bed, silhouetted against the moonlight from the window. 'Who is it?' she asked sleepily.

'It's Jennifer. Please, get up, I need help.'

At once Helen was struggling to get out of the bed and to don a dressing gown. In a minute she had a lamp lit.

'What is wrong?'

'It's Alicia, she's quite ill. I think the doctor should be summoned.'

Some of the alarm went out of Helen's eyes. 'Oh, that,' she said, adjusting the chimney to the lamp. 'Are you quite sure? Doctor Goodman does not like to be summoned all the way to Darkwater in the dead of the night, just for Alicia's spells.'

'I think this is rather more serious.' Something in her tone conveyed the concern she felt. For a moment Helen regarded her across the room. Then she seemed to accept what Jennifer said.

'Wait here,' she said. 'I will get Walter.' She slipped from the room with a rustling of silk and disappeared along the dark hallway.

*   *   *

Alone in her room, Alicia was tormented by fear, by her conviction that it was

189

wicked magic that was torturing her. She always wore a narrow ribbon about her throat but now even this seemed to strangle her. She clawed at it and tore it away, flinging it from her. Still she could not get air into her lungs. It was as if giant hands were slowly squeezing her neck, strangling the life out of her.

It's evil, that's what it is, she thought, gasping frantically. If only Jennifer would come back . . . if only one of them would believe me . . .

Suddenly, she knew they would never believe her, never — unless she somehow proved to them that what she said was true. And she knew, knew beyond any doubt, that she must get out of her sick bed, must go seek the cause of her torment.

'Dear God,' she prayed with all the fervor of a devout believer, 'give me the strength to rise from my bed.'

The prayer did seem to give her new strength. She struggled to get her feet free of the bedclothes. Slowly, laboriously, she swung them to the floor. Her chest heaved with the violence of her breathing, but at last she was out of the bed and standing.

She steadied herself for a moment, clinging to the edge of the big dresser. Moving cautiously, but with a strength born of desperate determination, she went out into the hall.

She avoided the front stairs. Jennifer might be there and in any case what she was seeking was to the rear of the house. She crept along the hall, to the back stairs.

Here she had to pause to rest, sitting on the bottom step while her heart pounded and her head swam. For a moment she nearly sank into unconsciousness, but she heard a distant murmur of voices and knew it was Jennifer and Helen and Walter, descending the front stairs, on their way to her room.

Fear that they would find her and make her return to her bed before she had done what she must do gave her the strength to rise again to her feet and, clinging to the banister, clamber laboriously upward.

The stairs were dark and it had been so long since she had moved freely about the house. Once she stumbled and would have fallen but for the railing. She stood, clinging to it, swaying weakly to and fro, and prayed for her God to give her the additional strength she needed.

At last she was at the top and she could move more easily along the hallway, until she came to the room she was seeking, the room in which Liza slept . . . if she was sleeping.

The room was dark, and it was a rule of the house that matches were not kept in the children's rooms, but there was a lamp with matches on the hall table. She lit the lamp with trembling fingers. Shielding the chimney with one hand, she entered Liza's bedroom.

Liza was asleep in bed. There was no question that it was her. She had turned facing the door and her face looked more than ever a child's face in sleep. Nor did Alicia believe she was faking the sleep. It was simply too genuine.

A wave of disappointment, so real it was almost a physical blow, swept over Alicia. She had been so certain Liza was somehow to blame for her illness. For a moment she nearly dropped the lamp. It seemed as if all the strength she had summoned to make this journey was now spent and she was not even sure she could continue to stand.

She sat on the wooden chair by the dresser, and as she did so, her eyes went down, to the floor. At once she gave a start as she saw the little rag doll there. She bent, reaching for it, and picked it up.

A cold chill went over her. It was crude, but it was a doll, like that hen-doll Liza had made, only this one was made in the image of a woman. It had a head, with a face of sorts, and hair, and arms, and a dress.

Alicia fingered the dress. It was made from a scrap of material from one of her old dresses. She recognized the print that had always been a favorite of hers, a double muscadine.

And the hair, black strands roughly fastened to the doll's head . . . could it be strands of her own hair, gathered somehow from her pillow. It was the same color as hers, the same texture.

She held the doll toward the light to

study it more closely, and saw for the first time the ribbon at its throat. It was one of her ribbons, there was no doubt of that, a blue one that had been missing for some days. But that was not what sent such terror coursing along her spine.

The ribbon had been tied tight around the doll's neck, as if to strangle it. For a moment it seemed to Alicia that the doll's button face was distorted in a grimace of pain and terror.

★ ★ ★

'But where could she have gone?' Jennifer asked, staring at the empty bed in Alicia's room. 'And how? She was so weak a moment ago she could hardly sit up, let alone walk around.'

'Well, she certainly is not here,' Helen said, a bit sharply. 'It is not the first time Alicia's spells have fooled someone.' She seemed to be criticizing Jennifer for sounding the alarm unnecessarily.

'If she was as sick as you say, she couldn't have gone far,' Walter said. 'Let's look around.'

They went through the downstairs rooms, carrying the lamp with them and even looking into the shadowy corners to assure themselves Alicia was not for some reason hiding there.

Jennifer had just begun to think she had been the victim of some sort of cruel hoax when they heard Alicia scream. It was a shriek of pure terror, and it came from upstairs.

★   ★   ★

When they reached the upstairs, Walter leading the way, they found Alicia lying unconscious on the floor, half in and half out of Liza's bedroom. Peter and Mary, awakened by her screams, stood in the doorway of their bedroom, looking wide-eyed at their mother's inert form.

'It's all right, children, back to bed,' Helen said. She shooed them firmly back inside their room and ordered them into bed again.

Jennifer knelt beside Alicia. 'She's fainted.'

'But what on earth was she doing

here?' Walter asked.

'Liza . . . ?' Jennifer said. She knew how Alicia felt, especially now, and there must be some significance to finding Alicia in this very room. Had she come up the stairs, summoning the strength from God knew what source, meaning to harm Liza while she slept?

The same thought must have occurred to Walter, and he turned as if to investigate, but at the moment Liza appeared, rubbing her eyes sleepily.

'What's happening?' she asked.

'Alicia is quite ill,' Jennifer said. 'She's fainted. You may go back to bed.'

Liza seemed not to hear. She stood where she was, staring without expression down upon Alicia, until Walter repeated Jennifer's order: 'Back to bed now, Liza.' With that she went.

'I'll carry her downstairs,' Walter said, lifting his wife's frail body in his arms.

Helen reappeared from her grandchildren's bedroom. 'I'll send one of the servants for Doctor Goodman,' she said. 'No doubt they are all awake by now anyway.'

As Walter lifted Alicia, something fell from her hand. He did not see it, but Jennifer knelt to pick it up.

It was a crudely made doll, fashioned from a sock, really, and clothed in a rag dress. It had what appeared to be real hair, if a bit sparse. Perhaps the most striking thing about it was the ribbon tied so tightly about its neck. Jennifer almost loosened it, but then she thought probably that had been done to give the doll a distinct head.

Why Alicia should have such a doll she could not fathom. She wondered for a moment if it could have had anything to do with her scream. But surely not, she told herself. She put the doll atop the hall table and followed Walter downstairs.

Nothing served to revive Alicia and she was still unconscious when, much later in the night, morning, almost, Doctor Goodman finally arrived with the servant who had been sent for him.

'She's probably sleeping,' he said, none too cheerfully, when informed that Alicia had not regained consciousness. When he saw her, though, saw the distortion of pain on her face and heard her labored breathing, his attitude changed.

'I was right, then,' Jennifer said, assisting him at the bedside. 'This isn't just another of her spells. She's really sick this time.'

'Yes, thank heaven you sent for me,' he said. 'She is really sick. Critically, I might say.'

'What is it?'

'I wish to God I knew.' He felt the thin wrist for a pulse.

Morning came. Jennifer watched the windows grow gray and then light. She started to pull the shades but the doctor stopped her.

'No, let the light in,' he said. 'We may as well see what we're doing.'

Jennifer could not see that they were doing much, however. She did not blame the doctor for that. He had tried any number of things, even resorting to steam inhalation in an attempt to clear Alicia's breathing passages. Nothing seemed to help. Her breath was a ragged gasp each time and her chest rattled with the effort of getting air into her lungs.

Now, his invention exhausted, the doctor could only sit by the patient, watching for some sign of response to the injection he had given her.

Finally, he said, 'Perhaps some coffee. Not for the patient, for me.' He sounded weary, not with physical effort alone, but with helplessness as well.

'I'll see if Helen has some ready'

She found Walter waiting outside the bedroom door. 'How is she?' he asked.

'She is still unconscious. She seems unable to breathe, as if she were being strangled. I'm afraid Doctor Goodman is stymied.'

In the kitchen, she found that Bess was up and had plenty of coffee brewing. Breakfast would be ready whenever anyone wanted to eat, she informed them.

Jennifer did not feel much like eating. She could only think of Alicia, weak as she was, somehow, for some reason, making that journey upstairs. Why had she done it, and what had made her scream as she had, a scream of pure horror?

'It won't do to make yourself ill,' Walter

said, helping her carry the coffeepot back to Alicia's room.

'I know, I'm fine, really,' she said, giving him a weary smile. 'I've been trying to think. Why did Alicia scream like that? What frightened her so?'

'We all know how she feels about Liza, and she was in Liza's room.'

'Yes, but why go there at all? She certainly went there under her own power, which must have required an incredible effort. And why scream? She has never before shrieked at the mere sight of Liza.'

Walter stopped to face her directly. 'Are you suggesting Liza did something to her?'

She had to say, 'No, I don't think that. Unless she is a very fine actress, Liza had certainly been asleep when she came to the door of her room.'

'You will call me if there's any change,' Walter said at the door to Alicia's bedroom.

Jennifer promised that she would and, taking the coffeepot from him, went in. Her heartbeat quickened a little when she saw the doctor bent over his patient.

'What has happened?' she asked.

'She was conscious for a moment,' he said. 'I thought she acted as if she wanted to tell me something, but her mind must have been wandering. All she talked about was a doll.'

'A doll? What doll?'

'I have no idea. She said it was her, and that it was killing her. Doesn't make much sense, does it?'

Jennifer did not reply. She watched in silence as the doctor tried to revive Alicia again, but she had sunk once more into that pained sleep.

Suddenly, so unexpectedly that it made Jennifer jump, Alicia's eyes flew open. She looked straight upward.

'My God, she's killing me,' she said. 'She's really killing me this time.'

'Mrs. Dere,' Doctor Goodman began, but he could say no more before she grasped at her throat with a low cry of pain. She seemed to be trying to tear something away, as if invisible hands were strangling her. Her eyes were fixed and as glassy as death.

Alicia gasped and closed her eyes again, writhing upon the bed, choking, strangling. The sounds that came from her throat now were unintelligible, inarticulate gurgles of fast-failing breath.

'You'd better call Mr. Dere,' the doctor said, feeling again for a pulse.

Walter was at his post outside when Jennifer opened the door. He looked at her with anxious eyes and she only nodded and motioned for him to go in. She knew there was nothing more she could do inside, and Alicia was entitled to those few seconds of life alone with her husband.

She went along the hall, but was startled to discover Liza, still in her nightdress, seated on one of the lower steps.

'What are you doing out of bed?' she asked, a bit sharply because she was very tired and her nerves were on edge.

'It's morning,' Liza said without expression. 'I always get up at this time.'

Jennifer had forgotten that the sun had come up. Although the windows had been open in Alicia's room, it seemed as if she had just left the black gloom of night.

'Is she worse?' Liza asked.

'She is dying.'

Walter came out of Alicia's bedroom. From inside, the doctor called after him, 'Get kerosene. Maybe that will cut the phlegm.'

Walter went to do his bidding and Jennifer sat on the steps beside Liza. Before Walter returned, however, the doctor came out of the room, head down, and closed the door softly. Coming down the hall with the kerosene, Walter saw him and paused.

'She is in the hands of her maker,' the doctor said.

Walter went into the bedroom alone. The doctor saw Jennifer and came to where she was now standing.

'Thank you for your assistance,' he said.

'I'm afraid I did very little.'

'Indeed. I did too little myself.'

'What . . . ?' She let the question go unfinished.

'What was wrong with her? I don't really know. Some sort of croup, I suppose. That's what I shall put on the certificate, but I don't really know. I never saw anything like it.'

When he had gone on to the kitchen, Jennifer remembered his remarks about a doll that Alicia thought was killing her. Could it have been the doll she saw upstairs? Her mind had been so occupied she had forgotten it until now.

She went up the stairs, moving slowly because she could feel fatigue weighting her limbs down. She'd had almost no sleep this night and she knew she should try to rest. The family would not need her now and this death was their private affair.

Still, the mystery of the doll bothered her. It was not on the table where she thought she had put it. She tried to think back, to envision the scene, but she found that she could not recall it clearly.

Maybe after all she had put the doll someplace else. Certainly no one would have taken it, unless one of the children had seen it and picked it up, in which case it would reappear in due time. And what if it did? She had no idea what significance it had, if any.

Despite her fatigue, she did not yet go to her room. She went downstairs again and out the side door, and stood in the shade of the magnolia tree there, breathing in the still cool morning air. Suddenly, quite without expecting to, she began to cry.

She was still crying softly into her hands when Walter found her and came up to her, putting a gentle hand on her shoulder.

'So, someone is crying for Alicia,' he said. 'I should have known it would be you.'

She dabbed at her eyes with the handkerchief he gave her. 'I'm not even crying for her, so much as for the fact that no one else is crying for her. No one loved her, no one is truly sorry she is gone.'

'I tried to love her.'

'I know that you did. I know that you tried to be a good husband to her, and I can cry too because she would not let you be. I see the sun above, and this tree here, and out there the swamp, and I tell myself that same sun shone on the earth when she was born. She walked beside those waters when she was a little girl, and happy, and loved. This tree was here the day she came to Darkwater as your bride. They are still here, and she has gone. Oh, Walter, I don't know, I suppose I am not making much sense . . . '

'Jennifer,' he said, and stopped, surprised with himself because he had never called her that before.

She heard it too, and was thrilled in her heart, and hated herself for being thrilled, now, on this day of all days, in the wake of this event.

'We had better go in now,' she said and, without waiting for his reply, she left him and returned to the house.

★   ★   ★

The funeral services were held at the house, and people came from miles around. Jennifer reflected ruefully that no doubt the 'witch' stories brought some people out of curiosity.

The Baptist choir sang 'Rock of Ages'

and the minister spoke briefly of the deceased. Staring at the woman in the casket, Jennifer had an eerie sensation once, as if she had seen Alicia's eyes open and staring at her. She blinked and saw that they were closed, but the feeling persisted, making her skin crawl.

She looked to the right and saw the old clock that stood there. It had not run, Helen had told her when she first came here, in forty years. Now, she would not have been surprised to hear the clock strike. Things felt as if they had slipped out of their natural order. But the clock held its peace.

At last the funeral was over, the casket lowered into the ground in the family cemetery. Jennifer had not spoken to Walter since that morning under the magnolia tree, except in a very business-like way. She had devoted her attention to the children, although in fact they were not in need of much consolation. They were young and for most of their lives their mother had not been a mother to them but rather a disquieting presence in the house. No doubt the fact of death awed them, and they were appropriately solemn around the family adults, but alone, out of doors, they were as high spirited and fun loving as ever. In that, Liza, who mourned not at all, encouraged them.

After the funeral itself, the house was filled with mourners and the church ladies who had brought food for the crowds. Jennifer had to admit that the air of somber cordiality was a relief after the deep silence that had settled upon the house in the wake of Alicia's death.

At last it was over. Only a nagging sense of something amiss lingered in Jennifer's mind. She had forgotten completely the doll that had so frightened Alicia the night of her death. She had not seen it to bring it back to her mind.

Now she did see it again. She had come to Liza's room to see that she, as well as the other children, was ready for dinner. There was a houseful of company and she did not want them to look ill-kempt simply because Helen was too busy downstairs to look after them.

'I think you could wear a fresh dress,'

Jennifer said when she saw that Liza was in one of the dresses she normally wore for play.

'I haven't anything to wear,' Liza said.

'What nonsense,' Jennifer said, going to the wardrobe. 'There are dozens of dresses in here.' She opened a door and saw on the floor the doll that had dropped from Alicia's hand the night of her death.

'What's this?' She stooped to pick it up.

'It's my doll,' Liza snatched it out of her hand. 'Give it here. I made it. It's mine.'

Her voice was rising and, fearful of a scene that would disturb those downstairs, Jennifer let it go. 'I think you should put on a fresh dress,' she said again, and left the room, her face burning. She knew that if she went to Walter he would discipline Liza for her rudeness, but she did not want to disturb him now with petty household quarrels.

Still, she wondered, through the dinner and even as the guests were departing — why should Liza be so excited about that doll? Why had Alicia been so excited about it?

Alone for a moment in the kitchen with Bess, she asked her, 'What does a rag doll suggest to you?'

'A rag doll? What kind of doll?' Bess asked, screwing up her face suspiciously.

'Just that. Made from a sock, with some hair attached to it and a ribbon at its throat. Alicia had it the night she died, when we found her upstairs, and I found it a bit ago in Liza's room, and it seemed to be important to both of them, but I can't imagine why.'

Bess was silent for so long that Jennifer thought she meant not to answer, and when she did, her answer was entirely noncommittal. 'It's probably just some old keepsake,' she said, turning back to her cooking, but Jennifer had the sense that there was something more she hadn't said.

★   ★   ★

When Jennifer did speak to Walter that night, it was briefly, and she had again forgotten about the rag doll.

She had gone to her room and finding

herself too keyed up to sleep, she went back downstairs to the library, in search of a book to read. She was surprised to find Walter there, seated in a big old wing chair.

'I'm sorry,' she said. 'I didn't expect anyone. I was just looking for a book to read.'

'Please, help yourself.'

She went to the shelves and hurriedly selected a volume, but when she started to leave with it, he stopped her.

'You needn't run away from me,' he said.

'I thought you would want to be alone.'

'Yes, I should be, I suppose. But I want to talk to you briefly, if I may.'

She turned toward him and waited in silence.

'I suppose you've wondered about your future, now that Alicia is gone,' he said.

She nodded. 'Yes, I have.'

'I still have the children, and they are more than my mother can manage. It would please us . . . it would please *me* . . . if you stayed on to care for them.'

'I shall be glad to stay, then,' she said.

Thinking he had finished, she started once more to leave, but again he stopped her.

'Miss Hale . . . Jennifer . . . ' He paused, looking suddenly embarrassed. 'I know this is neither the time nor the place to speak of . . . of certain things. Alicia's death. Her illness before that. These have been very sad for me, sadder perhaps than I show. But the dead must bury the dead, and the living must go on living. In due time, when Alicia has been mourned long enough to satisfy propriety, I would like to talk to you further. About the future. About our future. If you will listen.'

She knew that he had all but proposed to her, and despite the solemnity of death in the house, her heart skipped a beat.

'I shall be ready to listen whenever you want to talk.' Then, because she could not trust herself longer to honor discretion, she did leave him, practically running all the way back to her room, and flinging herself across her bed, to think of the future.

'Our future,' he had called it.

8

On Christmas Eve, Walter proposed to Jennifer, and she joyfully accepted. It had been more than six months since Alicia's death. Everyone knew that it had been a relief to Walter, as well as to the rest of the family, when Alicia died, and although the period of mourning had been brief, no one was shocked by the announcement of the engagement.

Indeed, there were many who were surprised that it had taken so long or that the couple, ever more obviously in love with one another, had been able to remain in such close proximity and yet remain so chaste.

It was not so difficult for Jennifer as many of the local women thought. It was true that with each day, as she became more aware of his strength and his goodness, she grew more and more in love with him. But to wait for that happiness was no sacrifice. She knew that she would be with him, and that was worth waiting for. Whatever impatience she might have felt was quickly negated by her dreams of what their happiness would be.

It was like a child's Christmas, all the more thrilling for having to wait, and in those months when he was respecting his dead wife's memory, no kiss was shared between them, no clandestine meetings held in darkened rooms, no secret messages shared. All that they did was done openly, before the eyes of his family.

Summer's brilliance faded gradually into autumn's softer splendor and with it faded the stark memory of Alicia. Winter came and the weather was cooler, although still much warmer than the winters Jennifer had known further north.

Thanksgiving was the first truly festive occasion in the house since Jennifer had arrived there, and although it was muted because Walter remained in mourning, it was still a happy occasion.

'After all,' Helen pointed out, 'we have much to thank the Lord for, and it would not do to forget that.'

After Thanksgiving, it was time to think about Christmas. Jennifer made a trip to New Orleans with Helen, Susan and Martin Donally.

'We have a house here, the old Oglethorpe house,' Helen said when they checked into their hotel, 'but it's hardly worth opening it up for a night or two.'

Jennifer was able to shop for things she could not find in Durieville. She bought a French parasol for Helen and a handsomely bound volume of Shakespeare's comedies for Walter, and of course, toys for Walter's children.

Liza was more of a problem. At first, in the weeks following Alicia's death, Liza had seemed genuinely happy, although she tried to subdue her feelings before the family. More than once Jennifer heard her singing gaily to herself, and she threw herself into her lessons with an enthusiasm that was infectious.

Gradually, though, she had begun to withdraw again. She stopped singing and gave up on her schoolwork until Jennifer threatened her with a scolding from Walter. It almost seemed as if Liza's happiness decreased as Jennifer's increased, until now they were back to where they had started, or perhaps further than that. There was almost an enmity between them that Jennifer, try as she would, could not dispel.

In the end she decided upon a dress for Liza, a rather grown up dress, Helen thought.

'Liza is probably almost fifteen,' Jennifer reminded her. 'And in due time there will be boys coming to see her, if Walter intends to keep her on at Darkwater.'

'It's been so long since we did much real entertaining at Darkwater,' Helen said a bit wistfully. 'Perhaps in the spring, we could have a party — a real party.'

'Perhaps,' Jennifer agreed, and smiled to herself because she already had in mind an occasion for celebration.

At last it was Christmas Eve. The children were sent to bed and Walter carried in the tree he had cut for the holiday. They trimmed it with the ornaments Helen brought from the attic, elegant crystals and brightly painted wooden figures, to which Jennifer added strings of popcorn and cranberries. When they were finished and Walter had affixed a gaily-painted angel to the top, it was very festive looking.

'Bess has some punch for us,' Helen said. 'I'll tell her to bring it in and have a glass with us.'

When she had gone, Walter came to where Jennifer stood just before the tree and put an arm about her. The move surprised her, for it was the first overt display of affection between them, but she did not move away or protest.

'Some time ago,' he said, leaning close to speak softly into her ear, 'I said that when the time came, I would like to speak to you about our future.'

She nodded mutely, unable to trust her voice. She wondered if he could hear the pounding of her heart.

'The time has come,' he said. 'I want you to marry me, if you will. And this is the present I have for you.'

He handed her a small box. It was unwrapped and it took no great insight to guess what it held. Slowly, she lifted the lid and there, nestled on a bed of midnight blue velvet, was the loveliest ring she had ever seen, a modest diamond surrounded by dainty chips of what looked like emeralds.

'It . . . it's lovely,' she murmured, staring at the ring in awe.

'Will you wear it? Will you be my wife?'

She turned in his arms, to smile up and him, and said, with tears glimmering in her eyes, 'Oh, yes, my darling, yes.'

He kissed her then for the first time and she knew that never in her life had she known what true happiness or joy was. She was drowning, drowning in his kiss, sinking into his arms, and a fire from within, that she had never known existed there, blazed to life, seeming to consume and purify her.

From somewhere far distant she heard a surprised Helen say, 'Oh,' but she no longer cared who saw them or what they might think.

At last, too soon, the kiss ended and she floated breathlessly back to earth and became aware of Helen and Bess, and behind them Susan and Martin.

'It's all right,' Walter said, beaming. 'We are going to be married.'

With that pandemonium broke loose and so great was the excitement that Christmas was almost forgotten. At last Susan said, 'Well, it looks as if this will be the first really merry Christmas in several years.' She did not say what they were all thinking — since Alicia had come to Darkwater as Walter's bride.

'Christmas, good heavens, I had all but forgotten,' Jennifer exclaimed.

They all laughed and Bess passed around the punch. They drank toasts and wished one another merry Christmas.

'Merry Christmas, darling,' Walter said, kissing her once again, but more discreetly this time.

'Merry Christmas, my beloved,' she whispered in reply.

'When will the happy event be?' Martin wanted to know.

'As soon as possible,' Walter replied. There was more laughter and some teasing at his impatience.

But Jennifer took a more sober view of things. 'It will take time to make preparations. Normally the father of the bride assumes the responsibility.'

'This wedding shall be my responsibility,' Helen said. 'My present to both of you. And it shall be the grandest this county has ever seen.'

'That alone will take time,' Jennifer said again. 'And there is the question of Walter's mourning. So it will be next summer, at least.'

'Too long,' Walter said. 'If my family and I think I have mourned long enough . . .'

Jennifer shook her head firmly. 'I'll have no wagging tongues at my wedding, and no bad luck. In June you will have mourned for a year. We can be wed in July.'

Walter gave in to her on this point, but said, 'Then I insist upon the earliest date in July. The first, or the second.'

'The second then,' Jennifer agreed. 'July the second, 1881. What a lucky day that will be for me.'

Midnight came and went, too soon it seemed to Jennifer, on this most wonderful of all nights. The evening drew to a close. Susan and Martin left to return to their cottage and Bess began clearing up.

Helen lingered for a moment, checking to be sure that all the presents for the children were under the tree. Then she too bade Jennifer and Walter good night and wished them a final Merry Christmas.

'Merry Christmas,' they replied in unison.

At last they were alone. Walter again took her into his arms. 'I wish it were now,' he whispered, kissing her once more.

'The time will pass.'

'Not quickly enough.' But he kissed her good night at her bedroom door as chastely as a boy bringing his sweetheart home from their first date.

Jennifer lay awake for a long time. She knew that the children would be up early and that she ought to get some sleep. Tomorrow was Christmas day, after all.

She, however, had already received the dearest present she could ever dream of.

★ ★ ★

Although Jennifer awoke at her usual early time, it was to find that the children had long since awakened and gone down to discover their presents under the tree. She dressed quickly and went to join them, taking special delight in observing their pleasure and happiness.

Each of the children thanked her for their presents and it seemed to her that even Liza had begun to melt a little.

'Thank you, Miss Jennifer, for the dress,' she said, holding it up before her. 'It's beautiful. And it's so grown up.'

Helen and then Walter soon joined them in the living room. The children thanked Helen somewhat soberly and Walter with many squeals and hugs. When Walter was finally disentangled and the laughter had somewhat died down, he went to where Jennifer was standing and put an arm affectionately around her.

'Now I have another present for you, children,' he said, beaming. 'A new mother. Miss Jennifer and I have decided we will be married.'

As Jennifer had expected, the children were somewhat stunned by the announcement. Mary and Peter looked, she thought, more pleased than not, and she felt that when they had time to reflect upon it, they would take it well. She was quite fond of the two youngsters and she knew they were attached to her as well.

It was Liza, however, about whom she was concerned, and she saw at a glance that Liza was not taking it well. Her eyes had gone wide with shock and she turned them briefly upon Jennifer with a look of incredulity.

'It isn't true,' she cried, running to Walter and flinging her arms about him. 'Tell me it isn't true, you're only teasing.' She began to sob.

Walter was taken aback by this outburst. For a moment he held her and patted her comfortingly, but when the crying and the protest continued, he suddenly took firm hold of her and held her at arm's length.

'Stop it. Stop it, I say. It is true. We are going to be married and you should be pleased for us. I think you owe Jennifer an apology for your rude outburst.'

'Walter,' Jennifer began, meaning to protest, but Liza ended the scene herself, at least for the moment. She twisted free of his grasp and before he could stop her, she ran from the room. They heard her footsteps clattering along the hall and up the stairs.

He moved as if he would go after her, but Jennifer laid a restraining hand on his arm. 'Let her go,' she said. 'She needs a good cry and to be by herself for a while. Later, when she's calmer, you can discuss it with her.'

He hesitated, obviously angry and embarrassed, but he relented with a wan smile. 'She'll get used to the idea,' he said.

Jennifer was not so sure of that, but at the moment her thoughts were of the other two children, Walter's own children, who stared wide-eyed in reaction to Liza's outburst. She did not want Liza's dismay to affect their reaction to the news.

'I'm sure she will. And in the meantime, let us not permit everyone's Christmas to be spoiled. Why, Mary, you haven't even opened that book. And, Peter, I don't believe I have seen you play with that new top.'

At her prompting the children went back to their toys and were soon engrossed in them. Liza was allowed to remain in her room throughout the morning. Jennifer's heart went out to her, on this morning especially, which ought to be a joyous one. How difficult it was to be in that stage between childhood and womanhood. A few years younger or older, and things would have gone so differently.

Bess had gone out of her way to prepare an especially festive Christmas spread. Later guests would drop by for a cup of punch, but dinner was reserved for the family and Martin and Susan, who came at midmorning to spend the day. They sang carols in the lavishly decorated front parlor. Jennifer played the piano and led the singing, and even Walter seemed to forget the day's bad start and join in the mood of merriment.

Later, when it was time to dress for dinner, Jennifer thought she would look in on Liza. Perhaps the two of them alone could talk more frankly. She had realized something for the first time this morning. Watching Liza's outburst, she had discovered that the girl's feelings were something more than a childish attachment. She had clung to Walter with a genuine passion and she had sobbed with all the despair of a heartbroken lover. She was sure that, in her girlish way, Liza was in love with Walter, not as a daughter loved a father, but as a woman, however young yet, loved a man.

She could never tell Walter this. She was sure that he saw Liza only as a child and looked upon Liza's attachment to him as a sort of father substitution.

Jennifer thought that if Liza could be made to understand that each of them had her place in Walter's feelings then perhaps she could accept his marriage with more equanimity. She must speak to her not as to a child, but as to a young woman and with complete honesty. And of course Walter need not know the full import of this 'girl talk.'

It was easy to excuse herself from the parlor. Helen and Susan had retired to look in on things in the kitchen. The children were busy with their new playthings, and the men were having one of their frequent arguments over the future of farming.

Jennifer slipped quietly from the room. The door to Liza's room was closed. She hesitated, wondering if she should intrude on the girl's privacy at this particular moment, but she knew she might not have an opportunity to speak openly in the near future. She tapped lightly on the door.

'Liza,' she called softly, 'it's Jennifer. May I come in?'

There was no reply, even when she knocked again, a bit more loudly. Thinking that maybe Liza was asleep, Jennifer opened the door a crack.

'Liza,' she called, but still there was no reply.

She went in, to find the room empty. Liza's bed was disarranged, where she had apparently thrown herself across it when she ran upstairs, but of Liza there was no sign. Jennifer remembered how distraught she had been and had a feeling of uneasiness. Could Liza have done something rash, something to harm herself?

Jennifer began to go systematically but quickly from bedroom to bedroom, until she had covered the second floor and found Liza nowhere. On an impulse, she went up to the attic. She took her time, looking behind trunks and into big, old armoires that had probably come from France. It was not impossible, she reasoned, that Liza would hide from her.

Her search of the attic revealed nothing and at last, increasingly worried, she descended again to the parlor, where the men were still arguing the future of the farm worker.

'Excuse me,' Jennifer interrupted them, 'I wonder if anyone has seen Liza?'

'Why, no,' Walter said. 'I thought she was in her room. Isn't she?'

'No.' The sound of her voice seemed to make him understand something of what she had been thinking. A frown darkened his handsome face.

'She's probably in one of the other bedrooms,' he said. 'I'll go find her. It's time I had a talk with her anyway.'

'I've already looked upstairs and in the attic. She seems to be missing.'

'Missing? I doubt she'd go far,' Walter said.

Jennifer knew that he had not gauged the depth of Liza's feelings for him and so could not comprehend what a shock his announcement had been.

'Walter, I am worried about her,' she said. 'I'm afraid she may have done something rash. She may have run away.'

'That's preposterous. She's just a child. She wouldn't run away.'

'She did once before.'

He looked at her in disbelief, but she looked so concerned that he gave in. 'We'll look for her,' he said. 'I feel sure she's around the house somewhere though.'

Helen and Susan were summoned and they made a quick search of the house, with no results. They made a brief tour of the grounds as well.

'We may be making a mountain out of a molehill,' Susan said. 'After all, Darkwater is quite large. There are a great many outbuildings and acres and acres of fields. Or she might have decided to go out for a stroll.'

Jennifer could see that the others, including Walter, leaned toward this view. She could not still her own fears, but she did not want to seem an alarmist either.

'It is possible,' she conceded. 'But surely then we can assume she will return for dinner, can't we?'

'You can bet on that,' Walter said, smiling. 'She loves to eat. Wait and see, just before dinner time she'll come strolling in from somewhere, surprised that we were worried and completely recovered from her little tantrum.'

As the time passed, however, Jennifer could see that each of the others was beginning to wonder. Finally it was time for dinner and Bess rang the great old bell outside the kitchen door. Its peals echoed over the dark waters of the bayou, but they did not bring Liza running for the house.

'Perhaps you've been right,' Walter said to Jennifer, his face more somber now. 'Get the help and let's make a real search of the outbuildings, the grounds, even the house again, just in case she has been hiding.'

Dinner was forgotten in the flurry of activity that followed, but even the thorough search of the house and grounds revealed no trace of Liza. It was no longer possible to pretend that she had not gone away.

'Want me to have the men start searching the bayou?' Martin asked.

Walter was thoughtful for a moment. 'No, I have another idea,' he said. 'If Liza has left here, there's only one other place she could have gone.'

'Where's that?' Martin asked.

But Jennifer already knew. 'She's gone back to Mrs. Hodges.'

'The swamp witch?' Helen said, unbelieving.

'She was living there before, when I found her. It's the only other place she knows around here,' Walter said. 'When she thought this was no longer home for her, she must have thought that was her real home.'

A cool rain had begun to fall and he dressed to go out in it. The other men did not offer to accompany him. It was as if they knew this was a personal journey, not to be shared with outsiders.

Jennifer thought of the cruel, old woman in the swamp, and she thought of Liza with her, subjected to the woman's violent temper.

'I'm going with you,' she said suddenly, running after Walter.

9

In the heavy rain the darkness of the swamp was intensified. It might almost have been night as they hurried along the path.

Walter led the way, cautioning her to stay close. He walked fast, once or twice consciously slowing his stride when she began to fall behind. Even so she had to rush to keep pace with him.

They reached the fork in the path and went to the right. As if it were an omen, the rain stopped suddenly, and the gloom seemed to lighten perceptibly.

'Where does that other path lead?' Jennifer asked breathlessly.

'Back to Darkwater,' Walter said without even turning his head. 'This path takes us directly to Mrs. Hodges' shack.'

'But when I came here before, Liza told me the path to the right would bring me back to Darkwater.'

'You must have gotten it confused.'

She was too short of breath to argue the point, but she was certain she had gotten it correct. Only, how could Liza, have gotten them confused? Unless she had wanted Jennifer to meet Mrs. Hodges. Unless . . . but no, Liza could surely not have wished her to be harmed. Or could she?

Like the others she had looked upon Liza as a child, an innocent. Yet, Jennifer had seen things — a look of malice in Liza's eyes from time to time, a wariness, a violent streak. Small things, but did they add up to a darkness of nature that no one had suspected as yet?

That was not entirely true, either. Alicia had suspected something. And Alicia was dead.

They arrived just then at the clearing where Jennifer had earlier encountered Mrs. Hodges, and Walter stopped so abruptly that Jennifer, following close behind, ran into him.

They had again come upon Mrs. Hodges in the clearing. The old crone stood directly in their path, just a few feet ahead of them. Walter wasted no time in coming to the point.

'We've come for the girl,' he said. 'Where is she?'

Jennifer's fear turned to puzzlement when Mrs. Hodges smiled, sweetly and innocently.

'She's at my place,' she said.

For all the sweetness of her smile, Jennifer thought it was enigmatic, too, as if she were pulling off some really outstanding stunt.

Walter must have thought the same thing. 'No tricks, now. We mean to take her home to Darkwater.'

'Darkwater?' She chuckled softly. 'Her home, is it now? My, my, we move up in the world, don't we?'

'It is her home, and I'm taking her back to it. Don't try to interfere.'

'Why of course she can go with you.' Mrs. Hodges showed a toothy grin. 'Supposin' she wants to. Maybe she likes it better here with her dear momma.' She let loose a cackle of laughter that set Jennifer's teeth on edge.

The crone was still laughing and watching them with an expression of amusement, but she made no move to stop them when they went by her.

'Do you suppose she's up to some trick?' Jennifer asked. She glanced back, but Mrs. Hodges had not moved.

'She gives that impression, doesn't she? We'll soon know. If she's harmed Liza . . . ' Jennifer could sense his fury. Again she wondered about the true nature of the relationship between man and child.

They came around a bend and Jennifer gasped. Directly in front of the path, a ramshackle house sat in a clearing, surrounded by a dilapidated fence. The yard was unkempt, the house itself unpainted. A pig wallowed in a pool of muddy water just inches from the crooked steps that led into the house. The front door was a screen, torn in many places and standing open at the moment. One of the windows was broken, only a few jagged spears of glass still clinging to the frame.

It was not the house, however sordid it was, that had made Jennifer gasp. It was the sight of Mrs. Hodges standing just inside the gate, awaiting their arrival.

'How did you get here so fast?' Walter demanded.

She chuckled again. 'I have my ways, boyo, I have my ways.'

It was difficult to imagine, Jennifer thought, that such an old woman could have come through the thick tangle of brush that surrounded the house and gotten here before them. No doubt there was a shortcut of some sort, but it was certainly well concealed.

'We still want the girl,' Walter said.

'Why, of course,' Mrs. Hodges said. She tilted her head and called, in a sing-song voice, 'Liza, come out. We've got company, child.'

Jennifer wondered how anyone accustomed to the comfort of Darkwater could come voluntarily to live in this filth and decay.

Mrs. Hodges called again, more firmly, 'Liza, come out now. There's nothing to be ascared of.'

Liza appeared in the doorway. She did not look surprised to see them. But of course, Jennifer thought, she must have known that Walter would come for her.

'We've come to take you home,' Walter said.

'Yes, I know,' Liza replied.

To Jennifer's surprise, Liza smiled and came demurely down the broken steps. It was difficult to believe this was the same child who had earlier thrown such a violent tantrum. Jennifer had expected some sort of sullen resistance, at the least, and perhaps more tears.

Liza came directly to Walter. 'I'm sorry for this morning.'

'I think you owe the apology to Jennifer,' he said.

Jennifer was certain Liza would balk at this, but she turned to Jennifer as humbly as anyone could ask and said, 'I do apologize.'

Jennifer was so surprised she could only stammer, 'And I accept your apology.'

Then, to further confound her, Liza burst into a smile and said, 'I'm so glad you're going to be married. I know you'll make Walter very happy.'

Behind them, Mrs. Hodges chuckled softly.

Helen often puzzled over the change in Liza. The wedding drew nearer, and Helen expected Liza to revert to her old resentment, but she remained a changed girl. She was astonishingly docile and good-natured. She even had a certain enthusiasm for the wedding and from time to time took part in the planning, encouraged by Jennifer.

That the two of them had become friends of some sort was obvious, for they were almost always together now.

To be sure, there were occasions when the old Liza re-emerged, although Helen thought that she saw more of that than the others. And sometimes Liza would disappear for hours. Usually this happened when Jennifer was not around, so Helen couldn't say Liza was avoiding Jennifer.

Jennifer, however, was more and more tied up as the wedding arrangements progressed. Often she had to go into town. Twice she and Helen traveled to New Orleans, which kept them away for several days each time. When she was at home, Jennifer was busy designing and making her own gown, preparing guest lists, and a hundred other details.

Now that she was to be Walter's bride and not an employee, she had to 'meet' the local people officially, which meant that she was often out calling.

On these occasions when Jennifer was out, Liza seemed to disappear. Once Helen saw her going into the swamp and another time emerging along the swamp path, but she could get no information from Liza.

'Where have you been all afternoon?' she asked.

'Nowhere.'

And again, 'Do you see Mrs. Hodges when you're in the swamp?'

'I never go into the swamp.'

'But I saw you returning, just today.'

'No. I never go into the swamp.' This was said with such calm certainty that Helen almost conceded she had been mistaken — but later, when she thought about it, she knew she had seen Liza coming out of the swamp.

Liza had lied to her. It worried her and she thought vaguely she ought to do something, but she did not know quite what. She had an uneasy feeling that if she punished Liza, Walter would take Liza's part. And if she went to Walter with her suspicions? She thought of Alicia, always telling Walter the bad things Liza was doing. Would she sound like Alicia, at least to Walter?

In the end, she did nothing, but the uneasiness remained. The girl was cunning. Could she be up to something?

But what?

* * *

Helen had little time to ponder these things, however. The wedding would be big and lavish, and it seemed there was hardly time now for anything but the wedding.

The wedding was scheduled for July the second, and people were coming from hundreds of miles away. The house would be filled with overnight guests and the sheds and outbuildings had been readied

241

for the children and the servants to sleep in.

A vast canopy for the ceremony itself was set up on the lawn. The reception was to be held inside. Helen had borrowed help from the neighboring plantations. An entire army of servants would be on hand to serve the guests.

'This will be the biggest to-do anyone around here has seen since before the war,' was Bess's opinion.

For Jennifer it was a heavenly period — all the details of the wedding to be arranged, under Helen's adept supervision; so many new people to meet and make friends with; the sensation of luxury, of money to spend lavishly; the travel. All of these kept her breathless and thrilled.

Most of all, there was Walter. No longer need they exchange meaningful glances at a distance, or dream fondly of one another from afar. Now they could stroll hand in hand around the lawn of an evening, or sit cozily close in the parlor.

At last June came, and with the glorious onslaught of summer, the wedding preparations entered their last frenzied stages.

Gowns had to be fitted and final adjustments made. Food arrived, seemingly from around the world, and all Darkwater was a giant madhouse.

Helen and Bess were everywhere all at the same time, overseeing everything, ordering Walter out of their way as regally as if he were a manservant. Bess herself was responsible for all the marketing. She traveled into New Orleans, where she purchased the fresh calves' feet from which the jelly was made. Stripped of their tough outer layer, they were cut up and then ground into a powder. Hot water and sugar were added to make jelly. Cochineal was added for the pink gelatin, spinach juice for the green, and thickened lemon juice for the yellow.

Weeks before, the most precious luxury of all, ice, had been loaded onto a steamboat far upriver, packed in straw to slow the melting. A special cellar had been dug and the ice was buried in more straw. Finally the jelly was set on the ice to harden.

The crude brown sugar made and used on the plantations was replaced with white refined sugar purchased on Bess's trip to New Orleans. It came in hard cones like rock and for days Darkwater rang with the sound of mallets breaking it into chips, which were then ground into fine powder.

Smoke stood up straight from the tall kitchen chimneys on the last few days of preparation. The ovens, great metal affairs with their tops filled with live coals, were pushed into the fireplaces. Everywhere pots simmered and steamed with roux and soups and gumbo. A giant, seldom used fireplace was smoking now and across its front the meats — wild boar and venison — turned on spits, spattering their juices into pots set on the hearth.

Orange blossoms and violets were dipped into boiling syrup and allowed to harden into candy. In the kitchen yard, ice cream custards had been poured into huge cylinders, which were turned continuously by strong black men. Every few minutes a man would give up his place at the tubs and sit back to blow on his freezing hands. If one rested too long,

Bess was there scoring him with her sharp tongue.

Knives were rubbed on a hardwood board covered with powdered brick dust, to sharpen them. The gelatins, hardened now, and the sherbets and russes went down into the ice cellar. Vast cakes were stacked in layers and iced in the pantry, with much finger licking. Orange peels were woven into delicate little baskets, to be dipped into the boiling sugar syrup and set to harden, when they would be filled with sweets — pralines and bonbons and nougats.

Walter chose the wines and liquors and set them on the sideboard, but even here Helen reigned, making countless suggestions until Walter gave it up with a toss of his hands and went back to his fields.

Flowers filled urns and vases and ramblers and hybrid roses from the garden garlanded the front staircase.

'I don't recall ever seeing anything this grand,' Susan said, watching in awe as the last details were attended to. She shook her head as the servants were brought in for Helen's inspection, wearing livery new from the skin out. Two small boys wearing turbans rehearsed standing on each side of the immense tables, pulling golden cords that moved the huge fans above.

'Surely everything must be ready by now,' Jennifer said, looking around with amusement and awe. It was June thirtieth.

'Almost,' Helen said. 'And you? Your dress is just right?'

'Perfect,' Jennifer said with a little laugh. 'You mustn't start in on me with your army of servants. I would be too exhausted to stand up for the ceremony.'

'Hmm. Well, you have gotten a tan from too much time in the sun. Sleep with some sour buttermilk on your face for the next two nights. And I will do your hair myself.'

'Let me trim it,' Liza cried. With each day she had been more and more at Jennifer's side, so that Jennifer had all but forgotten her old animosity. Almost, but not quite, because she could never quite get over the impression of something below the surface, something just out of sight, but menacing. Sometimes she had the feeling that Liza was with her not out of any desire for companionship but to watch her.

But then she would shrug and tell herself that she was being foolish. As if to quiet her doubts, she greeted each gesture of Liza's with even greater enthusiasm, trying to reassure herself of their new friendship.

So, when Liza asked for a scrap of the fabric from her wedding gown, Jennifer made sure to find her a piece, and when Liza asked to trim her hair, she readily agreed.

'Yes, let Liza trim it,' Jennifer said, seeing Helen was about to refuse.

'If you like,' Helen said in a tone that left it plain what she thought of that idea.

The night before the wedding, when Jennifer had all but forgotten her hair, Liza tapped at her door, scissors in hand.

'I've come to trim your hair,' she said.

Jennifer took a seat at her dressing table and Liza came to stand behind her.

'Helen says she will come and set it when I have finished. Are you excited about tomorrow?'

'Yes, of course. Aren't you?'

There was a pause. Jennifer glanced up into the mirror. Liza's attention was directed to her hair, so that she was unaware that she was observed, and she wore such a look of scornful malice on her face that it gave Jennifer a start.

'Don't do that,' Liza scolded. 'You'll make me ruin your hair.'

Jennifer looked up into the mirror then and Liza's expression was again sweet and faintly puzzled.

'What's wrong? Why did you jump like that?'

'Nothing.' Jennifer shook her head. Perhaps she had only imagined it. 'I'm just nervous, I guess.'

Liza frowned. 'That would be an omen. Mrs. Hodges taught me to believe in omens. Do you?'

'I . . . I'm not sure. For instance?'

'Well, for instance, if something really awful happened tomorrow, on your wedding day. It would be a bad omen. It would mean that your marriage was cursed.'

'Liza! What a thing to say.'

'It was only a for-instance. Or something really nice could happen. That would be a good omen.'

'Well, something really nice will happen. I will become Walter's bride. I think that you have cut it short enough.'

'Yes.' Liza bent down and began to gather up the strands of hair that she had cut, tucking them into her pocket.

'You needn't clean that up,' Jennifer said. 'The maids will do it.'

'Oh, I don't mind.' Liza continued to stuff hair into her pocket. 'Besides, I want a lock of your hair.'

'What on earth for?'

'Because we're friends now. It's all right, isn't it?'

'Yes, I guess so. Now go tell Helen I'm ready.'

★ ★ ★

'Ugh, it smells vile,' Liza said of the hair dressing, but Helen ignored her. She had already pounded beef marrow into a fluid state, and now she added thick castor oil.

249

Finally, she scented the concoction with oil of bergamot and patchouli and rubbed it into Jennifer's thick, black hair, twisting each lock into curl papers so tightly that Jennifer gave a little cry of protest.

Afterward, her lips smeared with a salve of white wax and sweet oil, her face smelling of buttermilk, Jennifer was escorted off to bed, to sleep her last night as a single woman.

When she was in her bed, though, her thoughts went back to Liza, and the strange contradictions in their relationship. Liza tried so hard now to be friendly. Not since Christmas and her temper tantrum had she done anything disagreeable.

Yet, there were moments . . . that face in the mirror, glowering savagely down at her head . . . had she only imagined that malice in the expression?

At one time she had reached the conclusion that Liza was in love with Walter. If that were so, had she gotten over her girlish love? Or had she somehow subdued it, for the sake of domestic tranquility?

Could she be harboring a bitter resentment that Walter was marrying someone else? Liza was not the sort, either, to harbor a resentment without acting on it. In her own devious ways she had acted against Alicia.

'Is she acting against me?' Jennifer asked herself. 'In some subtle way I don't understand?'

Now you are being a fool, she decided, and turned over, trying again to get to sleep.

★ ★ ★

Bess was surprised to see that a light still burned in Liza's room. She opened the door without knocking. Liza sat on the edge of her bed. At the sound of the door, she jumped and thrust her hands behind her.

'What you doing still up?' Bess asked, eyeing the girl suspiciously. Of all those in the house, she was the one least impressed with Liza's good behavior. She had an abiding distrust of her.

'None of your business,' Liza snapped.

'What are you doing, going around spying on people?'

'I thought I saw something shiny.' Bess came closer to the bed. 'And what is this? Hair? And this bit of cloth, why, that's off Miss Jennifer's wedding dress, I recognize the fabric.'

'She gave it to me. It was just an extra piece and she said I could have it to make a doll.'

Bess's dark face went darker still. 'What kind of doll you making? Let me see what you got behind your back. Give it here.'

She forced Liza's hand open. A golden chain fell to the floor.

'That's Miss Jennifer's pendant,' Bess said, picking it up. 'She's all the time wearing this. You goin' to tell me she gives you this, too, huh?'

Liza said nothing, only looked sullenly down at the floor.

Bess leaned close. 'What kind of doll you makin'? Is this some of that old swamp woman's mischief?'

Liza looked up then, her eyes flashing. 'I could make a doll of you too, you know,' she said.

Fear flickered in Bess's eyes and she could not quite conceal it. 'You could, huh? And I could just tell Mr. Walter too, couldn't I?'

'He'd never believe you. He'd laugh and say you were being silly.'

Bess took a step backward. Liza was right, those people never believed in the powers. The threat of having some evil power directed against her was beginning really to frighten her.

'Just see you don't practice any mischief around this house, or I'll see that you get into trouble,' she said, but the authority was gone from her voice.

'Oh, I won't,' Liza said with exaggerated sweetness. She held out her hand. 'May I have the pendant back? Please?'

For a moment their eyes met, and what Bess saw made a cold shiver run down her spine. She dropped the gold chain into the outstretched hand and, without a word, turned and went quickly from the room, crossing herself as she went.

10

Guests came from throughout Louisiana and even as far away as Alabama, staunch matrons whose daughters had been laced unmercifully into corsets with whalebone stays and pieces of applewood three inches wide up the front, so that no deviation could be permitted from the posture of a gentlewoman.

Stores in New Orleans and Mobile had exhausted their supplies of rice powder and the sale of imported Parisian gowns and hats hadn't been better since before the war.

★　★　★

Martin, Walter's best man, helped him dress for the ceremony. Walter had not seen Jennifer since the previous day. 'It's bad luck for the groom to see the bride,' Helen insisted, strictly enforcing her edict.

'Why, your hands are shaking,' Martin said.

'Well, yes, this is the biggest day of my life,' Walter said. 'I've been married before, of course, but not like this. This time it's the woman of my own choosing and I am marrying for love. This time will be forever.'

The ruffles on Walter's white linen shirt had been starched until they stood out stiffly from his broad chest. His new cutaway coat was dark maroon, so dark and rich that the color was only evident when the light struck it, and it was trimmed with mother-of-pearl buttons. His waistcoat was cream-colored with an embossed fleur-de-lis pattern, and the stocks were white silk, so soft and clear that they appeared blue in the folds. His boots were polished until they reflected the light of every candle.

Peter, who had been in an ecstasy of excitement for days, came running into the room.

'Poppa, they're coming, they're coming,' he squealed, trying to climb up his father's neatly trousered leg.

'Well, then, we'd better go greet them, hadn't we?' Walter said, grinning.

Peter ran ahead to join Mary. Liza, Jennifer's flower girl, was nowhere to be seen. Walter supposed she was with the bride-to-be. At the mere thought of Jennifer, his heartbeat quickened a little. Today, she would be his wife. And tonight . . .

Outside, footmen were opening the doors of the coaches. At the door, a butler called off the names of the guests as they arrived. Walter and Helen greeted them and they were led through the house to the wide back lawn, where tables of punch and hors d'oeuvres awaited them. From a pavilion nearby an orchestra played waltzes.

Wide as the lawns were, they seemed filled with beautifully gowned ladies and elegantly costumed men, moving gracefully about, standing in little groups and laughing and chatting.

Nevertheless there was a tension in the air. Each was waiting for the big event to begin and, at last, the time had come. At a signal from Helen, who had just re-emerged from inside, the orchestra broke off the song they were playing and began instead the wedding music of Mendelssohn.

The guests formed a great circle, all eyes turned toward the door through which the bride-to-be would emerge. The minister took his place under the canopy, and Walter and Martin joined him there.

Something between a breath and a vast sigh rose from the lips of all those present, hovering in the air like an echo, as Jennifer came from the house.

She paused for a moment, framed in the doorway. All of the blossoms, which decorated the tables, paled beside her pearly loveliness. She had, after all, defied the curls Helen had so carefully set and spurned convention. Every other woman there wore her hair in the customary style, parted in the middle, with bunches of curls on each side.

Jennifer, however, had brushed hers until it fell in heavy midnight cascades about her creamy white shoulders. She wore a gown of ancient French lace, which had been imported all the way from Paris, and it was cut in an extreme décolleté. She wore Helen's own fine strand of pearls. Only the loss of her golden pendant, which had been her mother's and which she had intended to wear, marred her preparations, but this had quickly been forgotten in the rush of getting ready.

Doctor Goodman had graciously requested, and been granted, the honor of giving the bride away. Helen was matron of honor and Liza the flower girl. Mary followed Liza with a pillow, which bore the ring Jennifer would give her husband, the ring that had been worn by her father.

When they reached the pulpit, Jennifer raised her eyes and looked into the face of her groom. She saw that he was bursting with happiness and pride and knew that all the effort and all the worry of preparation and dressing had been worth it. She felt as if she were floating on a pale white cloud. As if from a distance she heard the minister begin to speak.

But something was wrong. From the rear came an excited babble of voices, which others tried to shush, but the news, whatever it was, would not be quieted. It spread through the crowd like a flash fire through the brush, until the minister stopped speaking and everyone turned around.

'The President has been shot,' someone shouted. 'President Garfield has been shot.' Others picked it up like echoes. ' . . . Garfield . . . still alive . . . '

It took half an hour before the pandemonium died down and some sort of peace was restored. Stunned by the news and the disruption of her wedding, Jennifer had returned to her room.

'You mustn't let this upset you,' Susan said over and over. 'Things happen.'

'Yes, I know they do,' Jennifer said. She was thinking of Liza's remark the night before, about bad omens. 'If something really awful happened, it would be a bad omen . . . '

Well, this had been really awful, and surely it was a bad omen, on her wedding day.

At last Helen was able to restore order below and again the ceremony began, and this time it went without incident. But when at last the minister said, 'You may now kiss the bride,' and Walter took her into his arms, Jennifer could not escape a feeling of waiting disaster.

After the wedding, the guests came inside for a great feast. The ballroom had been turned into a dining room, with huge tables of carved mahogany placed in a semicircle.

They sat down and at once an army of servants began bearing in the turkey, goose, chicken, venison and the wild boar. There was so much that the guests could do little but touch each course, all the while admiring the silver epergnes of trailing flowers in the center of each table, and the side tables groaning under their burdens of salad and cold meats and the jellies, the iced cakes and the ice creams and the wines glowing in their crystal decanters. At each lady's place sat a basket of orange peel, filled with the candied petals of rose, violet and orange blossom.

Waiters moved continuously about the room, seeing that none of the precious goblets were allowed to remain half empty.

It was a feast such as had not been served in twenty years. Helen had spared nothing, neither creative effort nor expense, not because she was a showy, extravagant woman, nor because she had any particular desire to impress her neighbors. She was of a fine, old family and had no need to impress anyone.

She knew human nature, however. She knew that this was her son's second marriage, and that people around here who had not had to live with Alicia had a great respect for the woman. Alicia had died in what might be termed mysterious circumstances, and Jennifer, Walter's second wife, had been living here at the time. Even after such a long wait, she knew tongues would wag.

She had done all she could to forestall this by seeing that Jennifer met all the important women hereabout, knowing that Jennifer's natural charm would help her greatly in winning their approval.

She had reckoned too that this return to the opulence of the past would so overwhelm these ladies that they would relinquish their gossip and bend to

Jennifer as an important social influence locally. These were women who thrived on luxury. A bride who could command such a wedding would by necessity be respected by them.

She had not counted on help from outside, however. The shooting of the President had redirected everyone's gossip even more effectively than the splendor of the wedding had. When the ladies left that day, they were whispering among themselves — she observed countless curled heads bent together — but it was not of Walter's marriage to Jennifer they talked.

They talked of the President and whether he would live or die, and how and why he had been shot. Men at the party had sent their servants into town for news, and some had even left themselves, offering their excuses to their hostess.

'It was an omen,' Jennifer had said darkly while they waited for the uproar to cease so the wedding could resume.

'What nonsense,' Helen had replied. 'Now you're talking like Bess, with all her fear of witches and black magic and the like.' But privately, she had to admit, it was not an auspicious beginning to a marriage.

As to Bess, with her enormous workload now mostly behind her, she was thinking of a friend she knew that she should visit. Auntie Doreen, she called her, though they were not in fact blood relations. Auntie Doreen was an authority on the black arts. Bess had decided that she might have need of her expertise.

* * *

It was a less auspicious beginning to Jennifer's marriage than Helen realized.

Alone in their bridal chamber, in the room that had been Walter's bedroom, Jennifer had looked forward with tremulous passion to this first night in her husband's arms.

Walter had brought up a bottle of champagne and some glasses, and he poured a glass for each of them.

'To us, and to our many happy years together,' he said, raising his glass in a toast.

Jennifer raised her glass too, but her

hand shook, partly with excitement and partly with the nervousness that had lingered after the unfortunate disruption of the wedding ceremony.

It suddenly seemed to her that the room was intensely cold, although it was a midsummer night. The shadows in the room danced about her, leaping out from the corners where they had been crouching. She could not get her breath. It felt as if hands were at her throat, suddenly squeezing . . .

When she regained consciousness, she was in bed, the bed that had been prepared for her wedding night with Walter. He leaned over her, a glass of water in his hands.

'Feel better now?' he asked.

'I . . . ' She could not seem to collect her thoughts. 'What happened?'

'You fainted,' he said. When she started to sit up, he forcibly held her down. 'It's all right. It's just all the excitement, and probably a bit more wine than you should have had. Mother did herself up proud, didn't she?'

His efforts to change the subject did

not lessen her feelings of concern. 'But Walter,' she said, her mind finally beginning to clear, 'I didn't drink at all. I only put my glass to my lips. You know I hardly ever drink wine. And I felt fine all day until . . . until just before it happened.'

'It's all right,' he told her again, leaning down to kiss her forehead. 'You get some rest now. I'll sleep right here in the chair.'

Her protests were to no avail. Nothing would do but that he had to sleep in the chair, and at last she stopped trying to convince him otherwise and allowed him to put out the lamp.

Lying in the darkness, she was haunted by an ugly thought: Just like Alicia. This is just like what he had with her.

★　★　★

In the morning Walter insisted upon sending for Doctor Goodman, who came and, to Jennifer's further disappointment, prescribed a few days in bed.

'But, really, doctor, I'm not sick,' she protested. 'I feel well except for this odd choking in my throat.'

'Nervous spasm, perhaps,' he said. 'All the excitement of the wedding, crowds of people, that business with the President. No, you stay in bed for a few days, and keep yourself away from the children until we see just what's what.'

'Do you think it's something contagious?'

'It's best to take no chances until we're sure. It won't hurt to rest for a few days. If that husband of yours becomes a nuisance, you tell him to see me.'

Far from being a nuisance, Walter was a model of patience and solicitude. Jennifer remained in bed for four days and Walter could not find enough to do for her, until she began to feel like a pampered darling.

I can see how a woman would want to remain in bed and convalesce like this, she thought on the fourth day, and that thought had no sooner formed in her mind than she had a feeling of dismay.

When Walter came into the room next, he found her up and getting dressed, and when Doctor Goodman came to examine her, she said, 'Walter had one invalid to coddle, he needn't go through that again.'

After another examination the doctor conceded that there was apparently nothing wrong with her and Jennifer took up for the first time her role as Walter's wife.

She did not tell him, however, or the doctor, of the lingering pain in her throat or the shortness of breath that accompanied it.

★   ★   ★

For all the bad omens, things went rather well for a time. Her strange lingering illness was an inconvenience but not so severe that she was incapacitated. Walter was a wonderfully loving husband in his way. He was not a particularly demonstrative man and she knew she would rarely hear sweet nothings whispered in her ears, but his presence at her side was evidence of his love for her and she was content with that. If only she could be free of her pain long enough to truly enjoy their marriage — but she kept that resolutely to herself.

They had planned to leave for their honeymoon the morning after the wedding. Helen still owned her family home in New Orleans and Walter had suggested they go there for a few weeks.

'New Orleans is not what it was before the war but it's a lovely city nonetheless,' Helen said. 'It'll be a nice place to get away for a spell.'

Jennifer's illness had necessarily postponed the trip, but when she was out of bed they decided to go belatedly — and the first difficulty with Liza arose.

When the suggestion was first made, that Liza go with them, Jennifer tried not to be too argumentative about it. 'It is a little unusual, taking someone along on a honeymoon,' she said.

'But it's not as if it were really our honeymoon,' he pointed out. 'I mean, we have been married two weeks now. That makes a difference, don't you think? And anyway, Liza's had no opportunity to get away from here since she first came.'

There were several answers to that, Jennifer thought, although she did not make them aloud. In the first place,

Darkwater was not exactly at the end of the earth. And so far as Liza's leaving Darkwater, that was something Alicia had suggested rather strongly numerous times.

She was not surprised that Liza would ask to go. After all, for all that she was growing up, she was still half a child. She was a little more surprised, however, that Walter had agreed so readily.

In the end, she went along with the arrangement because she did not want to start out her marriage being disagreeable. She had already followed in Alicia's footsteps with her unexpected and mysterious sickness. To follow that up with a lot of quarreling over what was really an unimportant issue seemed mere folly. After all, Liza would not be sleeping in their bed. They would have plenty of time to themselves.

★ ★ ★

Since the town house was rarely used, there were only two servants in residence — Atlas, an old black man, and his sister,

269

Eugenie, both of whom had been with the family for years.

'You'll have to take help with you,' Helen pointed out. 'You'll not be able to get any there and Atlas and Eugenie are both along in years.'

So when finally they departed for New Orleans, two young women, Belle and Zerline, rode on the back of the carriage. Since Jennifer and Walter were in agreement that they would live simply while they were there, they anticipated no difficulties on that score.

It was a day's journey and it was evening by the time they arrived. Although they had come into the city for shopping before, always staying at hotels, this was the first time Jennifer would have a real opportunity to see the city.

She found it charming, although the filth always shocked her. She knew there were periodic outbreaks of yellow fever and cholera, because the water was polluted and the sanitation was poor.

The streets were twisting, mere lanes really, for the most part innocent of any pavement. Here and there stretches of broken cobblestone started and stopped with no apparent logic. Narrow sidewalks of brick, called *banquettes* by the Creoles, lined either side of the street and clung to the fronts of the brick and plaster houses.

Deep ditches, lined with cypress wood, lay between banquette and road. Trash and sewage were regularly dumped in these open, water-filled ditches. As the carriage rolled through the darkening streets, Jennifer saw the bloated carcass of a dog, dead several days, floating in the gutter. She looked quickly away.

The houses they passed had no walks or verandahs or even any sort of façade, but were built down to the very edge of the streets. When a person left the house he went from inner privacy to the bustle of the street with one step. Most of the houses, though, did have galleries, over-hanging balconies rich with wrought iron ornamentation, and these provided the passengers on the banquettes below with some protection from sun and rain.

Finally the carriage came to a stop. Walter alighted and, handing Jennifer and Liza down, he walked to a massive oaken door, lifting the iron knocker and letting it fall. While they waited, two nuns all in white passed by and smiled at them.

They heard footsteps from within. To Jennifer's surprise, the big door stayed closed and another, smaller one, cut within the large one, swung open instead. An old and tiny black woman, her apron stiffly starched, and wearing a red and blue and yellow tignon on her head, made a stiff curtsy and stood aside for them to enter.

'*Bon soir*, Monsieur Walter,' she greeted him, her French accent impeccable, and to the ladies, 'Watch your step here, it's very high.'

The passage within was cool and dark, and stretched before them fully fifty feet. Walter introduced the woman as Eugenie and presented Jennifer and Liza to her. She did another curtsy, and led the way down the corridor. It was paved with blue-gray flagstones, and the moldering walls were peeling in places, here and there revealing patches of bare brick. The ceiling was high overhead and beamed.

At the end of the passage they entered into a large courtyard paved with more of the blue-gray flagstones. Bamboo grew in large pots and an immense banana tree rustled in the faint evening breeze. In the courtyard's center, smaller pots of blooming oleander surrounded a gently splashing fountain. Balconies ran around three sides of the courtyard and stairs painted a faded green and festooned with a purple-flowered wisteria vine went up the fourth wall.

A tall black man came to meet them, bearing a candle. 'Good evening, Monsieur Walter,' he greeted them.

'Good evening, Atlas. This is Mrs. Dere, and this is Liza. I trust we won't be too much work for you while we are here.'

'Not too much for me, Monsieur Walter. I put those two girls you brought to work. Will you be having dinner?'

'Shortly,' Walter said. 'I think the ladies would like to freshen up a bit first.'

'Indeed. If you will come with me, Mesdames.'

They walked through the cool rooms with their immensely high ceilings. Jennifer could see that the furnishings were magnificent and so highly polished that they gleamed even in the dim light. Crystal chandeliers tinkled softly.

'This is lovely,' Jennifer said. 'Why haven't you lived here?'

'Because I don't care much for the city,' Walter said frankly. 'It's noisome, for one thing, and filthy. Every year or so there are outbreaks and half the population dies off. You'd think they'd leave and never come back, but they don't seem to. Besides, in the country we can sustain ourselves well. Even the Deres are less wealthy since the war. And being isolated as we were, we were hardly touched during the war. People here lost much. This house was looted once, but they didn't take the large things and the servants drove the soldiers away before they could do too much damage. If you look, you'll find bullet holes in some walls, and a shortage of small ornamental pieces.'

* * *

As they were weary from travel, they retired soon after dinner. Walter led

Jennifer through a maze of rooms and up sweeping flights of stairs to the master bedroom. It was a huge chamber, richly decorated, with a massive, canopied bed in its center.

It would have been the perfect setting for their belated honeymoon but for one difficulty. When Liza was shown to her room at the opposite end of the hall, she found that she was too much alone, and frightened in this big, unfamiliar house.

'But she has lived in the swamp,' Jennifer pointed out when Walter explained this to her. 'And at Darkwater she sleeps in her own room. I don't see why she should be frightened here.'

'It's all new to her,' he said. 'And she's only a child.'

Not so much a child, Jennifer thought, that she can't fend for herself quite well at home. But she chided herself for being uncharitable, and said, 'Well, the thing to do is to let one of the servants sleep in her room with her.'

Walter looked a little embarrassed. 'Actually,' he said, 'she asked if she couldn't just sleep in here with us until she got used to the house. I said it would be all right.'

'Walter,' Jennifer said, truly shocked at this arrangement, 'On our honeymoon . . . ?'

'Except it isn't, really,' he pointed out again, with maddening persistence. 'And it's not as if it will be our only night to sleep together. We have a lifetime ahead of us, my darling. This will only be for a night or two.'

Jennifer was prevented from arguing further by the arrival of Liza herself, in her nightgown which, Jennifer noticed, was already too small for her. Her legs, losing some of their adolescent gangliness, were rather generously revealed, almost to the knees. In a woman it would have been a shocking display. Jennifer thought it a bit immodest even for a girl.

'I don't want to be any trouble,' Liza said. 'I can just wrap up in a blanket and sleep here on the floor.'

'You'll do no such thing,' Walter said. 'You can sleep in the bed with Jennifer and I'll curl up in that chair.'

'But you'll get no sleep that way,' Jennifer said.

'I'm used to sleeping anywhere. Besides, it will only be for tonight. Tomorrow we'll find another bed and have it moved in here.'

Jennifer stilled her objections and went to bed, but she could not pretend to enjoy a honeymoon with her husband sleeping nearby in a chair and Liza, dropping off at once to an untroubled sleep, in bed beside her.

11

Liza never did quite get over being afraid in the new house. For the rest of their visit, she shared Jennifer's bed and Walter slept in the big chair, or in the adjoining bedroom. At first, Jennifer had argued about the arrangements, but nothing she said seemed to change Walter's way of thinking.

It was almost, she thought more than once, as if he were in a trance of some sort, or bewitched. But that sounded too much like the sort of things Alicia used to say, and she quickly dismissed that notion from her mind.

Perhaps she would not have minded so much had she and Walter been able to make up for it otherwise with time to themselves, but the fact was, they were never alone. Liza was with them constantly, and Walter was so conscientious about doing this or the other to entertain and please her that Jennifer began to genuinely resent Liza's presence.

I feel as if Walter and Liza are on a trip together, she told herself in the mirror one evening, *and I am along as a companion.*

Afterward, though, she would chide herself for her petty jealousy, and try again to enjoy the trip. Certainly Liza was enjoying herself, and she could not really blame Walter for sharing and even encouraging her high good spirits. She had never seemed quite so much a little girl.

On Saturday they had been invited to a party at the Harrows. At the last minute (why not sooner, Jennifer wondered?) it was discovered that the dress Liza had intended to wear was much too small for her.

'She's just grown too much these last few months,' Walter said. 'She's going to be a woman soon.'

In some ways she already is, Jennifer thought, but aloud she said, 'She is still young for a party such as the one the Harrows are giving. It won't hurt anything for her to stay home this evening.'

'By herself?' Walter looked shocked.

'Not entirely. There are servants in the house, Walter. And she has surely been here long enough by now to be used to the place.'

With some reluctance Walter explained that he had already promised Liza she could go. 'I can take her to one of the shops and buy a ready-made dress, and we can be back in plenty of time to get ready for the party.'

'But you will have to leave me alone in the house to do so,' Jennifer said drily. She did not wait for him to reply, but left the room.

In their bedroom, she brushed her hair before the mirror and tried to argue herself out of a bad mood. She assured herself that Walter's interest in Liza was entirely innocent. He was like a father to her. Still, it seemed to Jennifer that he was obsessed with the girl's pleasure. It really was as if he were possessed.

Well, a fat lot of good it will do me to sulk, she said to her reflection. *If I threatened not to go, they would only go without me, and I really would be left home by myself.*

They were a bit late to the party, but not unduly so. Jennifer wore a new gown, too, which had been selected for her trousseau. It was gray, and when she saw the vivid red dress Liza had selected, she thought hers made her look rather old and matronly.

Liza's dress added years to her age, too, but becomingly so. A woman could not have gotten away with wearing so bright a dress, one cut with so many skirts and ruffles, but at Liza's age it was enchanting. She looked perhaps seventeen, lost somewhere between innocence and seduction.

Jennifer could not help noting Walter's warm approval when Liza came running and whirling down the stairs in her new gown.

'I shall be the envy of every man there,' he said. Then, almost as an afterthought, he smiled at Jennifer and added, 'with two such lovely ladies as my companions.'

'I just know it's going to be a wonderful party,' Liza said as they entered the carriage to depart, but for Jennifer, the evening had already been spoiled.

By the time they arrived, the dancing was in full swing. Every man young enough to twirl and sashay, and some who were not, had captured himself a partner and was cutting a lively figure. The voluminous skirts of the ladies swirled and dipped.

It was a pretty sight, Jennifer thought. Except for her wedding she had not been to a party since she had been a very little girl. Despite herself, her spirits perked up. Her eyes sparkled and her cheeks glowed with pleasure.

The Harrows did not have a reception line. Guests came in unannounced and when the host or hostess saw them, they were introduced around. It was a more modern and more informal way of entertaining, and Jennifer found that she liked it better than the old way.

She had hardly been introduced around when her host asked if she would like to dance. At a nod from Walter, she consented and at once was whisked to the floor. She had not danced often since she was a girl, and she felt a bit stiff in contrast to the others dancing so lightly all about her. She saw Walter's eyes following her, however, as though he approved, and after that she relaxed a bit.

When the reel began, she asked Walter to come dance with her.

'Our host seems to be enjoying himself highly,' he said. 'And I'm not much of a dancer. Why don't you dance this one with him as well?'

Jennifer was a bit disappointed, but she took her place for the reel with Mr. Harrow.

Liza had been spirited from them almost as soon as they arrived, and she was with a group of young people who were dancing among themselves at one end of the room. Jennifer looked that way once while she was dancing, and could see at a glance that Liza resented being thrust off with the children instead of being allowed to remain with the adults. She looked bored and irritated, and looked longingly in Walter's direction.

As the reel began, a group of the youngsters swarmed toward Walter, clamoring that they too wanted to do a reel.

Liza was, it seemed, left without a partner, although she had been dancing only a moment before. Jennifer saw her seize Walter's hands and pull him into the dance. It looked as if he needed no urging.

The way he danced was a further revelation. She had never seen a man dance better. Like many big men, he was light on his feet, and Liza, her ruffles flashing crimson on each turn, was like blown thistledown.

Soon after the dance had begun, everyone else stopped to watch them. It was a lovely sight, people agreed with one another, the way they danced together.

Jennifer stood quite still and stared at them. She had not dreamed Walter could dance like that. Only a moment before he had declined to dance with her and now there he was with Liza, the center of all attention, object of all admiration. Liza came tripping down the line, her tiny feet seeming hardly to touch the floor.

Walter took her hands to pull her out of the dance. He did not even glance toward his wife. Jennifer turned and walked away.

She excused herself to her host, saying that she did not feel well and was leaving early.

'But your husband . . . ' he said.

' . . . Is still dancing. Good night and thank you for inviting me.'

The carriage was waiting. The driver looked surprised to see her so early and alone, but he said nothing.

She was already in her nightdress, brushing her hair for bed, when she heard the sound of another carriage outside and a moment later Walter's footsteps rushing up the stairs.

He burst into the room, looking frantic. 'Darling, what happened?' he cried, 'I thought you were ill.'

She heard Liza's lighter footsteps hurrying along the hall. She did not even have the privilege of quarreling with her husband in private.

Before Liza reached the room, Jennifer said, 'Walter, I think it is time Liza returned to Darkwater.'

'Liza? Why . . . ?'

'Because we are on our honeymoon, belated or not,' she said. She met his puzzled look with such an icy glare that he did not even attempt to question her further.

Liza came in to stand beside him. Again Jennifer had the impression that the two of them were together and she was an outsider. *She knew him before you came along*, a voice said within her.

'What's wrong?' Liza asked. 'Why did we have to leave so early? I was enjoying the party.'

'I was not,' Jennifer said. 'Good night.'

* * *

Whether some burst of insight had suddenly made Walter understand the cause of Jennifer's anger, or whether he merely decided not to risk testing it further, he told Liza in the morning that he was sending her back to Darkwater.

'After all,' he said at breakfast, 'you're supposed to be giving Helen a hand with the younger children.'

Liza took this decision darkly. She said little but there was no mistaking her sullen look, and once Jennifer caught a glance from her that seemed filled with threat.

Despite Liza's sulking, Walter stood firm in his decision. Having gotten what she wanted, Jennifer maintained a discreet silence on the subject. When Liza remained the entire day in her own room, of which she apparently had lost her fear, Jennifer half-expected that Walter would relent and let her stay on a little longer. Before retiring that evening, however, he instructed the servants to prepare the carriage for travel the next day and to pack Liza's bags early in the morning.

During the night, Jennifer was taken ill again. It was a sudden attack, and quite severe. One minute she was asleep, dreaming pleasant dreams, and the next, it was as if a cord had been tied around her neck and pulled tight.

She was awake in an instant, struggling for breath and clawing at her throat. There was nothing there but the collar of her nightgown, yet so real was her impression of something tied there that her fingers continued to scratch at the skin as if loosening something.

Walter woke and in alarm lit the lamp. He ran for Atlas and sent him at once for a doctor, but by the time the doctor had arrived, the spell had passed.

'I can find nothing physically wrong,' the doctor said after examining her.

'But, doctor, I didn't imagine it,' Jennifer said, her voice rising a little. She was thinking of Alicia. This was the same sort of spell she had, and the doctor had been unable to find anything wrong with her either. Jennifer could not even look at Walter. She wondered if he were thinking that history was repeating itself.

'Perhaps it was strain,' the doctor said. 'You've recently married, your husband tells me. You're away from home, no doubt more active than usual. Perhaps you've used your voice a great deal.' In the end, he could do nothing but give her a sedative and advise rest.

The following day all of them returned to Darkwater.

'You think I'm crazy, but just wait,' Alicia had said.

But Alicia had not been talking then about her illness. She was talking about

Liza. Jennifer glanced over at the girl, sitting on the other side of Walter. In a sense, Liza had gotten her way. She was not remaining in New Orleans, but then neither was Walter remaining to enjoy it without her.

*　*　*

Afterward, Jennifer seemed never to be quite well again. She forced herself to get out of bed as much as possible, but no effort of will could resist the fact that she was getting worse. Each week she convalesced more and more, spending first part of a day in bed, and then an entire day, and then two or three days in succession.

Again and again Doctor Goodman came and examined her and shook his head. He did not accuse her of anything but she could see silent reproach in his eyes.

'But, Doctor, this is exactly like Alicia, isn't it?' she said to him. 'You could find nothing wrong with her and you can find nothing wrong with me. And the symptoms are the same as she described hers. But my illness is real, not imagined.

The pain is real, and the difficulty in breathing.'

He shrugged and said, 'You could call in another doctor, of course. Frankly, I am at my wit's end.'

Walter was patient and kind, and yet in his eyes she could see a distant sadness, as if he too were thinking, we have been through this before.

Not until she saw Alicia did Jennifer begin to suspect anything approaching the truth.

It happened at night. She had been asleep and woke for no particular reason that she was aware of. She lay awake, listening to the sound of Walter's breathing and staring up at the ceiling.

Suddenly, she looked toward the door, and Alicia was there. She was clawing at her throat, just as Jennifer had seen her do so often, just as Jennifer herself had done during her recent 'spell.' It made Jennifer's skin crawl.

Alicia came toward the bed. She was holding something in one of her hands, and as she got closer, Jennifer recognized it. It was the rag doll Jennifer had seen the night Alicia died, the doll with the ribbon tied around its neck. Jennifer had forgotten it entirely since she had seen it in Liza's cupboard.

Alicia came still closer, until she was by the bed, and for the first time she opened her eyes and looked into Jennifer's. Jennifer shivered with fear. She had never experienced anything like this before. She had heard of people who saw ghosts, and she had always scoffed at them.

'She's a witch,' Alicia said in a voice exactly as Jennifer remembered it. 'You thought I was crazy, but I wasn't. She is a witch. She killed me and now she is killing you.'

Jennifer turned toward Walter to shake his shoulder. 'Walter, wake up, please,' she said.

'Huh, what . . . ?' He opened his eyes.

'Alicia, she's here,' Jennifer said, but when she looked again, Alicia had disappeared.

Walter was really awake now. He sat up and looked around. 'What do you mean, Alicia? Where? How?'

'She was here. Right beside the bed.

She spoke to me.' He gave her a peculiar look. 'I didn't imagine it. She was here.'

He sighed and lay back down. 'You were dreaming,' he said, as if that settled it, and went back to sleep.

She did not sleep for a long time, however. She kept remembering the way Alicia had looked, and the things she said. What did they mean?

'She is killing you.' Who, and how, and why?

Was Walter right? Had she dreamed it? Even if it was a dream, though, it must mean something, something dredged up from the deepest corners of her mind.

At last, unable to come to any satisfactory conclusion, she fell asleep again. Her dreams were troubled, but when she woke in the morning, she did not remember them.

★   ★   ★

It was one of the mornings when Jennifer was able to have breakfast with the family and Walter told the others of Jennifer's dream.

Jennifer was embarrassed, but she tried not to quarrel about it. 'It certainly seemed real,' she said when he asked if she was ready now to admit that it was only a dream.

'If she spoke, what did she say?' Helen asked.

'I don't remember,' Jennifer lied. She remembered quite well, but the children were at the table and listening quite intently to the conversation. She exchanged glances with Helen, who understood and tactfully changed the subject, to Jennifer's relief.

Jennifer did not really believe it had only been a dream — or, if it had been, it was meant to give her some kind of message. She knew the others would laugh at her if she insisted upon that, nor did she feel inclined to tell them what Alicia had said, which would only further provoke their amusement.

One of the listeners was not amused, however. Bess listened with wide eyes and later, when Jennifer had gone to her room, Bess came up to see her.

'Miss Jennifer,' she said, wringing her

hands and looking extremely nervous. 'I know it ain't my place, but I got to talk to you.'

'Why, of course, Bess,' Jennifer said, 'you know you can say anything you like to me.'

'You've been so good to me and all, even sticking up for me that time with Miss Alicia, it wouldn't do for me not to say something. Only, I don't know how to say it.'

'Say what?'

'And Miss Alicia coming to see you like that, I believe it was an omen, that I was supposed to tell you.'

She leaned forward, and said in a whisper, 'Miss Jennifer, she's killing you.'

'You mean Alicia?' Jennifer asked, startled. It was so like the words Alicia had used last night.

'No, I mean that girl, Liza.'

'But, good heavens, what can you mean? Why, she's only a child. Even assuming she would want to do such a thing, how could she? Do you mean she is poisoning me?'

'No, she's got a doll. Miss Jennifer, I

know you think I'm crazy or imagining things, but that girl lived in the swamp with the witch, and she learned her bad ways. She's got a doll, and they put a power on it, and what they do to that doll happens to you. I saw the doll, made to look like you, with your hair attached to it and everything. That's how she's making you sick.'

For a moment Jennifer could only sit and stare at her. A doll? Magic powers? Liza, wanting to kill her? It was all so incredible . . . and yet . . .

'If there is such a doll,' she said aloud, 'then we have only to present it to Walter and tell him everything. I shall call him.'

She started toward the door but Bess caught frantically at her arm. 'Oh, don't, please, don't. If she knew, she'd get me too. And anyway, it wouldn't do no good. He wouldn't believe it. He'd think I was crazy. You're thinking that yourself, don't you see?'

It was true, Jennifer thought, Walter would think she was mad if she came to him with such an outlandish story. She thought of Alicia, insisting that Liza was a witch. Everyone had thought she was mad. Would Walter be any more likely to believe this story, coming from Bess?

'But if what you say is true, what can I do?'

'My Auntie Doreen, she said if you could find the doll, take it away from her, take it all apart — but that wouldn't stop her from doing another one.'

'Still, it would buy me some time. If it's in her room . . . '

'It's no use. I looked in her room when Liza was outside yesterday, I was so scared, but I couldn't find it. Wherever it is, she is sure to have it hidden.'

'Did your Auntie have no other suggestions?'

Bess hesitated. 'She said . . . she said that the evil power comes from the witch woman. She says if we could stop her . . . '

'But how do we do that?'

'She said . . . ' Again Bess hesitated. 'She said with this.' She produced a small ceramic bottle from the deep pocket of her apron.

'What is it?'

'It's a witch's bottle. We have to collect things of hers. Some of her pee, if we can get that, that's especially powerful. But her hair, nail clippings, a bit of her clothing. Same as with the dolls, almost. And we put them in this bottle, and put a stopper in it, and we bury the bottle out in the yard.'

'And . . . ?'

'And she'll die. The swamp witch. It's the only way to kill her.'

12

The next day Jennifer felt so much better that she was inclined to dismiss not only her illness, but Bess's outlandish story as well. Even if Liza did have a doll made in her image it did not mean that the doll had any sort of evil power. It was probably only something Liza had used to frighten Bess.

It was a particularly hot season, and as the field work was caught up, Walter had promised the children he would go swimming with them at the boat landing, where the water was deep and cool.

'I think I will come and sit in the shade,' Jennifer announced. Walter seemed pleased, as did and Peter and Mary, but Liza was less than enthusiastic.

'There's no good shade down there,' she said.

'Then I shall take a parasol.'

Since it was only Walter and the children, he and Peter swam in their undergarments and Mary and Liza wore old dresses that had been cut off. Liza's, Jennifer observed from the landing, revealed quite a bit of her legs. It was modest enough out of the water, but when it had gotten wet, it was a blatant reminder that Liza was growing into a woman.

Walter seemed not to notice. He splashed and frolicked with all the children, but when he discovered that Liza did not know how to swim, nothing would do but that he must give her instructions.

I never realized that Liza was such a slow learner, Jennifer remarked to herself, observing the lack of progress as time went by. Peter and Mary had gone off to play by themselves and still Walter worked with Liza. She was fine when he held her, but whenever he let go of her she at once forgot what he had told her and splashed and kicked helplessly until he had to 'save' her.

Watching them, Jennifer felt more and more a coldness growing within her. Suddenly Liza did not look like a child at all but like a very lovely young woman.

Walter's back was to her, and Liza was in his arms. Briefly, Liza looked toward Jennifer and their eyes met.

Sometimes a glance is enough for communication between two people. It had happened with Walter. Jennifer had looked into his eyes and knew that he loved her. And now it happened in reverse with Liza. Their eyes met and in that instant, Jennifer knew that Liza hated her and that in some dark way she could not yet understand, Bess had been right.

She had been sitting on a hay-bale that Walter had placed for her. Now, as if stung by a bee, she stood. The movement caused Walter to look in her direction.

'I . . . I think Liza was right,' she said. 'There is not enough shade here. I am going back to the house.'

Walter scrambled to his feet. 'Wait, I'll come with you,' he said.

'No, don't, please. I'd rather you stay and enjoy yourself with the children.' She emphasized the last word deliberately and saw out of the corner of her eye that it was not wasted on Liza.

When she was out of sight of the swimmers, she ran the rest of the way to the house. Her heart was pounding, and not from the physical exertion alone. Without pausing as she entered the house she ran directly up the stairs, straight to Liza's room.

A doll, Bess had said. She began to search the room. She went through the drawers of the dresser and through the big wardrobe in which Liza's dresses hung. She found nothing.

She was on her knees looking under the bed when she heard a noise and looked up to see Liza standing in the doorway.

'Are you looking for something?' Liza asked, coming in and closing the door after herself.

Jennifer stood up, brushing her skirt. 'Yes,' she said, 'I'm looking for a doll.'

'I don't have any dolls. I'm too old for dolls.'

'I think you do have one. One made supposedly in my image.'

Liza's smile vanished. 'That damn cook! I'm going to make her sorry.'

'So you do know what I'm talking

about. I want that doll. Where is it?'

For the first time Liza looked full at her without any pretense. 'You'll never find it,' she said.

In the face of her naked hatred, Jennifer took a step back. 'Liza,' she said, actually frightened, 'You truly do hate me, don't you? I never realized it before. But why?'

'Because you married Walter. He should have waited for me. But I'll fix you.'

'I have had enough of this. If you will not show me that doll, I shall have Walter get it from you.'

'He'll think you're crazy. Just like his first wife. I'll say I know nothing about any doll. He'll never believe you.'

Jennifer stopped at the door. 'You're forgetting, Bess saw it.'

'If I threaten her, she'll deny she saw anything.'

Jennifer knew she dared not back down or Liza would forever have an advantage over her.

'We shall see,' she said. She found Walter in their bedroom, combing his hair before the mirror.

'Walter,' she said, not even pausing to greet him, 'I want Liza sent away.'

He gave her a shocked look. 'Why?'

She could see already that he had withdrawn from her but fear and anger drove her on almost hysterically.

'Because she is making me sick. She's a witch.'

'A witch? What on earth are you talking about?'

Before Jennifer could say anything more, however, Liza herself ran into the room and threw herself into Walter's arms, wet dress and all.

'Oh, Walter, Walter,' she sobbed, crying against his chest, 'It's all so stupid. I had a rag doll I made, and I wanted to scare Bess, so I told her it had magic powers. And now Jennifer believes her.'

Walter patted her shoulder and looked angrily past her at Jennifer. 'I hope you realize how foolish all this sounds,' he said.

'Perhaps to you. Not to me.' Jennifer's cheeks burned because in truth she could see that it sounded more than a little foolish. 'If there is nothing to it, then let her produce the doll. That's all I asked of her.'

'Well, little crybaby,' Walter said, holding Liza at arm's length. 'How about it? Let's see this wicked invention of yours.'

'But that's the whole trouble,' she sobbed. 'I don't have it. I lost it ages ago.'

Again Walter looked at Jennifer as if to say, *you see.* 'Well, if she doesn't have it, she could hardly be doing any mischief with it.'

'*If* she really doesn't have it. I think she's lying.'

Again he held Liza at arm's length. 'Cricket, I want you to tell me once and for all, and no fibbing. Do you have some sort of doll?'

'No, I lost it.'

'Then that is that,' he said. 'I hope we have no more of this.'

Jennifer's determination wavered in the face of his stern anger. She knew that Liza was lying, but without evidence she would never convince Walter. She started from the room.

'Don't you think you owe Liza an

apology?' Walter asked.

'No,' was her reply.

★ ★ ★

That night she had another of her spells, this one the worst yet. She lay gasping for breath, her fingers instinctively clawing at her throat, and all she could think of was the doll she had seen before, of Alicia, with the ribbon tied tightly about its neck.

'I've sent for the doctor,' Walter said wearily, coming to kneel beside the bed.

'Walter, that girl, she's a witch. Send her away, please,' she begged in a whisper.

He looked down at her coldly. 'You sound exactly like Alicia.'

★ ★ ★

By morning Jennifer knew what she must do. There was one person who could tell her if Liza possessed some sort of evil power — the person from whom she would have learned it.

She would go to see Mrs. Hodges.

There, she would either confirm what her instinct increasingly argued was true, or disprove it once and for all.

She was well enough in the morning to get out of bed and dress without help. She did not want anyone to know where she was going. Walter was in the fields and Bess and Helen were at work in the kitchen and she did not see Liza or the children, so she was able to steal from the house unobserved. Outside, she paused to get her breath.

What if she hadn't the strength for the walk through the swamp?

Inside, she heard Liza's voice, calling to one of the other children. It gave her a chill.

'I must find the strength,' she said.

Looking back on that time with Walter, Jennifer remembered Mrs. Hodges' sardonic amusement. Had she known then what Liza's return to Darkwater would mean for Jennifer? *And how will she greet me this time*, she wondered? *With amusement? Or violently?*

She hurried on, ignoring the shortness of breath that ached in her chest and the tightness at her throat. She no longer dared let herself think of those things, for fear that her mind would snap altogether.

She reached the shack — and standing before it, as if waiting for her, was Mrs. Hodges herself.

'Why, dearie, hello,' she said, giving Jennifer a toothy grin. 'Look at who's come to visit me. Are you out of breath? Let me give you a hand. That's it, up the steps. There, now, it's cooler in here, isn't it?'

It was the first time Jennifer had been inside the shack, but the outside appearance had prepared her for what she would find inside. It was filthy and squalid, with litter and trash strewn everywhere and the smell of rot and decay. At Mrs. Hodges' insistence, she seated herself in a battered stuffed chair. Dust rose in a little cloud as she sat, making her shudder with revulsion.

'There, now, that's better, isn't it?' Mrs. Hodges crooned, all tender solicitude.

'Thank you,' Jennifer gasped. For a moment she could only lay her head back and struggle for breath. She could see the cracks in the ceiling and thick cobwebs in the corners.

'Here, dearie, drink this' Mrs. Hodges appeared at her side with a cup.

'What is it?' Jennifer eyed the cup warily.

'It's an herb tea I brew. It'll make you feel better. And I should know, shouldn't I?'

Mrs. Hodges thrust the cup under her nose and Jennifer sipped obediently. The tea was hot and had an odd, bittersweet taste, but it was not unpleasant. It seemed she could actually feel it restoring some of her wasted strength. She took another sip and managed to sit upright.

'What is it?' she asked again.

'I had it brewing for you,' Mrs. Hodges said, ignoring the question. 'I knowed you was coming to see me.'

'How . . . how did you know?'

The woman gave her eerie chuckle. 'I knowed, is all. I know everything. I knowed you was sick, and how and why. It was me told her what to do.'

'You mean Liza? Your daughter?'

The chuckle changed to a snort of

scorn. 'Daughter? She ain't no daughter of mine. An ornery little whelp, came crawling in out of the swamp, wanting a place to sleep and something to eat. And I took her in, I did, took care of her, told everyone she was my own daughter. And now there she is up at that big fancy house and here I am sitting in this shack, me that taught her everything she knows.'

Jennifer forced herself to look into those wildly gleaming eyes. 'And it was you that taught her how . . . how to make me sick?'

Again the face broke into that cruel grin. 'Yes, yes, it was me did that. She come running back here, crying about this man she loved, and she'd gotten rid of one wife and now he was taking another, and would I help her again? And I says to her, I says, when you went up there, you was gonna fix it so I could come and live there too, and then you forgot me after I helped. So I says, now you want me to help you again.'

She paused and thrust the cup of tea at Jennifer again. 'Drink,' she commanded, and Jennifer drank obediently. The tea was making her feel oddly light-headed.

'So she whined and sniveled,' Mrs. Hodges went on, 'and said, she'd see I was comfortable this time, and I give her the things she wanted, and she brought the stuff down here and I made her the doll like she asked.'

Here she broke off into another chuckle and thrust her face so close to Jennifer's that her vile breath made Jennifer's stomach give a warning turn.

'That was a doll of you, sweetie.' She laughed loudly. 'It has power, that doll! That's how she's been making you sick, and it's all my doings, and now that I've helped her, I'm still sitting here in the swamp and she's up in that fine house, and I haven't seen her since. The ungrateful whelp.'

She suddenly straightened and took the cup away, waddling toward the kitchen area.

'And now you want my help too,' she said from the kitchen pump.

'I only wanted to know . . . '

'You only wanted to know,' Mrs. Hodges mimicked. 'You wanted to be rid of that brat, that's what you wanted! I knowed you was coming today, and I knowed what you was coming for. And I got it ready.'

She came back to Jennifer and handed her a small bottle filled with a purplish liquid. 'Here.'

'What is it?'

'A potion. You put that in your man's drink, or his coffee, and it'll make him come back to you. And it won't harm him none, either.'

Jennifer did not know what to say. She was frightened of the old woman and anything she might do, but the mere thought of reviving Walter's love for her was a siren's song that seemed to whisper in her ear, *take it, take it, take it*.

'Never you fear, it'll do what you want it to do. And here, here's something else I fixed up for you.'

She reached into a deep pocket of her dress and brought out an object. Jennifer started to reach for it and then brought her hand back.

'It's one of those dolls,' she said, horrified.

'It's her, Liza,' Mrs. Hodges said. 'In her image. Whatever you do to it, it will be done to her too. Take it.'

She dropped it in Jennifer's lap. Jennifer's instinct was to cast it away, but at the same time she was fascinated. She picked it up. It was like any child's rag doll, except that the hair was real, and she did not have to ask whose it was; and she recognized the rag dress as a scrap from one of Liza's dresses.

'Does it really have that sort of power?'

'Whatever you do. If you took a pin, for instance, and stuck it through there, where the heart is . . . '

Suiting action to words, she took the doll from Jennifer and, grabbing a huge pin from the nearby table, started to thrust it through the doll.

'No,' Jennifer cried, grabbing the doll away. 'It would kill her.' She knew then that, no matter what reason tried to tell her, she believed fully in the power of the dolls and their black magic.

Mrs. Hodges laughed. 'Take it. Keep it. Use it if you must.'

Jennifer remembered then what Bess

had told her, that the only way to truly remove the danger was to kill Mrs. Hodges, by burying that little bottle. But she couldn't do that, or kill Liza, either. No matter what kind of magic it was, that was still murder.

It suddenly seemed to her as if the filthy room were closing in on her. The smell of decay, Mrs. Hodges nasty breath, the dust, were all at once threatening to overpower her.

'I must go.' She struggled to her feet. 'I shall send someone with money to pay you.'

'I don't want your money, dearie, just your friendship. Never you fear, the tea will give you the strength to get back home.'

Oddly enough, Jennifer found her strength had come back. At the door, she paused. Mrs. Hodges had not moved.

'Yes, what did you forget?' she asked.

'The doll, the one Liza has in my image. How can I stop its power? How can I prevent her from making me ill and perhaps . . . perhaps worse?'

'Oh, that's very simple.' Mrs. Hodges

hobbled toward her. 'I'll show you.'

She pointed at the doll in Jennifer's hand. 'You take that doll there, the one I just gave you of her, and you stick a pin through its heart, right here, and she won't trouble you no more.'

Jennifer gave a little gasp of horror and flung the doll on the floor. She turned and ran from the shack, down the broken steps and into the waiting swamp. Mrs. Hodges' evil laugh echoed behind her.

13

Not until she was almost back to Darkwater did Jennifer realize that she still clasped in her hand the tiny bottle of liquid Mrs. Hodges had given her. She stopped and lifted her hand, meaning to fling the bottle into the dark water near the path.

Instead, she lowered her hand, staring at the bottle. What if it worked? Mrs. Hodges' tea had worked, hadn't it? Her progress going there had been a prolonged labor, but she had nearly run all the way home.

And what would she not do to bring Walter back to her? Mrs. Hodges had said it was harmless — but could she be trusted?

Slowly, Jennifer put the bottle into her pocket. She could always throw it away later, after all. She would wait and see.

She was surprised when she arrived back at the house to discover that she had already been missed and that her absence was the cause of some consternation.

'Heavens, there you are,' Helen greeted her, rushing into the hall. 'We've been frantic.'

'I just wanted to go for a walk,' Jennifer said. Bess was standing behind Helen, and for a moment her eyes met Jennifer's, and it was if some unspoken understanding passed between them. Bess nodded her head almost imperceptibly and Jennifer realized Bess knew where she had been, and that Mrs. Hodges had given her something. It seemed that Bess was telling her, *yes, go ahead, use it.*

'A walk?' Helen looked incredulous.

'Yes, I'm feeling much better today and I was tired of spending all my time in bed. Is Walter in?'

'Liza suggested that perhaps in a delirium you had wandered into the swamp, and at her suggestion they went to look for you.'

But not, Jennifer thought at once, *by the usual path or I would have met them.*

'Well,' she said aloud, 'I am home now and quite all right. I wonder if someone would bring some coffee up to my room, I think I would like some. And, Bess, send two cups. When Walter comes in I'll ask him to have some with me.'

Again, she had the impression that Bess understood more than had been said, but Bess only nodded and said, 'I'll bring some right up.'

'You do look as if you're feeling better,' Helen said in a puzzled tone. 'Do you want me to help you up the stairs?'

'No, I can manage.'

In her room, changed into her filmiest peignoir and waiting for Bess to arrive with the coffee, another thought struck her. Was she feeling better because of the odd tea Mrs. Hodges had given her, or because Liza was out and not tormenting the doll? It no longer struck her as remarkable that she would accept one or the other of those two possibilities.

Bess brought a tray bearing a steaming pot of coffee and two cups. 'I made the coffee real strong,' she said, setting the tray down near Jennifer's chair.

When Bess had gone, Jennifer took the little bottle from her pocket and turned it about in her hand. It gleamed in the light from the window like a liquid amethyst. She removing the stopper and held the bottle to her nose. It had almost no scent — so, presumably it would have little flavor as well.

She heard muffled voices from outside followed by the sound of steps along the hall. Walter was home and coming to see her. Quickly, she emptied the bottle into one of the cups. By the time Walter came into the room, she was pouring the coffee. She looked up and gave him a nervous smile.

'Hello, dear,' she greeted him.

'So you're back,' he said, not returning her smile. 'Where were you?'

'Just out for a stroll and a breath of fresh air. I didn't dream I would cause so much excitement.'

'You had everyone very worried. Liza and I have been out hiking through the swamp. She had an idea she had seen someone going that way and thought it might have been you. She was worried too.'

'Was she?' Jennifer asked, trying to

keep any sarcasm from her voice. 'I am sorry to have alarmed her. Come sit down, won't you, darling, and have some coffee with me.'

'I've got work to get back to,' he said, still in an ill humor.

'It can wait five minutes, surely,' she said in her most coaxing voice. 'And if you've been hiking around, you must be tired. It's been a while since you sat with me.'

Reluctantly, he came and sat in the chair opposite her. 'Your hands are shaking,' he said as she handed him one of the cups.

'Perhaps I was not as well as I thought. Drink it while it's hot, please.'

She lifted her own cup and tried to sip the strong brew, but it left a bitter taste in her mouth. What if that old witch gave me poison, she thought? The woman was certainly half-mad. She watched Walter lift his cup to his lips and for a moment she almost cried out.

Then the moment was past, he was drinking the coffee and it was done, for better or for worse. She gave a sigh and sank back in her chair.

He frowned down at his cup. 'It has an odd taste.'

'It's very strong. I asked Bess to make it that way.' She forced herself to drink some more. 'I rather like it like this.'

She watched him drink more of his and after a moment some of the stiffness went out of his posture. He seemed to relax visibly and when he looked at her again, his mouth formed itself into a smile and there was a tender light in his eyes that she had not seen for too long a time.

'I haven't been in very good spirits lately, I guess,' he said. 'I'm sorry. Will you forgive me?'

She set her own cup aside and said, smiling, 'Only if you kiss me.'

He knelt before her and took her in his arms. His lips sought hers, gently at first and then with a sudden intensity of passion. Eagerly she clung to him, her body melting against his, her lips warm and yielding. Her fingers moved through his hair.

'Darling,' she breathed hotly into his ear, 'must those chores be done just now?'

'But you've been sick,' he said, starting to draw away from her as if he had just remembered.

She held him tightly to her. 'And I am better today, so very much better.'

For a moment more he hesitated. Then he kissed her again, more passionately than before, and she knew that now a stronger magic was at work.

'Lock the door,' she said in a breathless whisper.

He did so and came back to take her in his arms again. He did not, apparently, hear the footsteps in the hall outside, as she did, or see the doorknob turn tentatively. The footsteps disappeared — in the direction of Liza's room.

She clung to him and tried to ignore the awful pain that began a moment later in her throat. Mrs. Hodges' tea had worn off, or Liza was at work on her doll again, but for the moment it did not matter. Let Liza do what she could, for now she would lie in Walter's arms, would die in them if she must. For the moment, Walter was hers, and not all the power of hell could change that.

* * *

Never had the pain been so horrible — yet Jennifer smiled through her agony as she thought of the cause of Liza's anger. It had been worth it, whatever it cost her in the way of suffering. And the look on Walter's face when he kissed her and went out, that was worth any price.

A fresh wave of pain broke over her and despite her efforts not to, she cried aloud. It felt as if her body were being broken on the rack. She tried to seize the bedpost, to hold herself steady, but she was too weak to grasp it and her hand fell limply across the sheet.

A sudden stab like a bolt of lightning went through her and she screamed, loudly. Then, mercifully, she fainted.

When she woke, Helen was there, bathing her face with a cold towel.

' . . . Too much for traipsing around out of doors,' Helen was saying. 'I thought that was too sudden a recovery. She should never have gotten out of bed.'

'Walter,' Jennifer gasped. Her voice was nothing more than a hoarse croak.

'He's gone out to the fields,' Helen said. 'They're harvesting the cane. Do you want me to send someone for him?'

'No, leave him there,' Jennifer said, clutching at Helen's arm for emphasis. 'I want . . . I want some of your special tea that you made for me before.'

'Of course.' Helen looked over her shoulder at Bess. 'You know how to make my tea, and . . . '

'No, you make it for me, please. It's never the same when someone else makes it.'

Helen sighed and although she looked harried, she was obviously flattered too. 'For heaven's sake, yes, I will make it myself. You'll be all right for a few minutes?'

'If Bess will stay with me.' Bess nodded and came to stand by the bed. The door opened and closed.

'Is she gone?'

'She's gone,' Bess said. 'And you look like you almost are too.'

'She's killing me,' Jennifer said in a fierce whisper. 'I think this time she's actually killing me. She's stabbing me

323

with . . . something.'

She gave a gasp as another sharp pain shot through her abdomen. In genuine terror now, she reached up and seized Bess' wrist.

'Bess, you must help me.'

'What can I do?' Bess asked, looking as if she were about to cry. 'I don't know how to stop her. I tried to find that doll, I looked everywhere, but she's too clever for that.'

'There is someone who can stop her,' Jennifer said. 'Mrs. Hodges. You must go for her, Bess, bring her here.'

'The witch?' Bess's eyes looked huge in her face. 'Bring her here? Miss Jennifer, I couldn't. I couldn't even go there.'

'Bess, you must. Look at me. Can't you see I am dying? And you are the only one who knows why or would believe me.'

Bess wrung her hands frantically and Jennifer could see the tears in her eyes. 'Miss Jennifer, I'm afraid.'

'And so am I,' Jennifer said with a wan smile. 'Bess, Bess, if there were anyone else — but there isn't. You *will* go?'

'I'll go, Miss Jennifer, but if I don't come back you'll know something awful happened to me.'

Helen brought the tea Jennifer had asked for, setting the tray down on the table near the bed.

'Here is your tea,' she said. 'And Jennifer, don't be angry, but I sent for Walter. He'll be here any minute.'

As if on cue, Walter's footsteps echoed down the hall and a moment later he burst into the room.

'Darling, I thought you were better,' he said, rushing to the bed and falling to his knees beside Jennifer. He embraced her gently but fervently.

'It's my fault,' he said, stroking her hair.

'Hush,' she whispered, patting his shoulder. 'If your love can't cure me, what can?'

And it was true, as if by magic she had begun to feel better in his arms. The pains had stopped shooting through her and suddenly she could breathe again. She took a deep breath, and felt new strength flowing into her limbs.

'You see,' she said, smiling up into his

face, 'at the touch of your hands I am already better.'

'I will never leave your side again,' he said passionately.

'Oh, hello, Walter,' Liza said from the doorway. 'I thought I heard you come in.'

Jennifer felt a chill go over her. This was why her pain had temporarily subsided. Liza had heard Walter come in and had stopped torturing the cursed doll to come here instead.

'Hello, Liza,' Walter said without looking at her. 'Jennifer's sick again. That's why I came back.'

'With all of us here to take care of Jennifer when she has her spells? The cane won't wait, you know.'

'As long as Jennifer needs me by her side, that's where I will be,' Walter said.

Neither Helen nor Walter was looking at Liza at just that moment, so only Jennifer saw that she was confused.

Liza was quick to recover, though. She's like a cat, Jennifer thought, landing on all fours no matter how she is thrown.

'Well, Jennifer looks as if she is better now,' Liza said. 'I think what she needs is a few hours of good sleep. Don't you agree, Jennifer?'

Jennifer saw the challenge in her eyes. Was she being offered a deal? Let Walter go for a time and Liza would let her rest without disturbance.

'If I could sleep,' she said cautiously, 'I would certainly welcome it.'

'Why don't you try, then? I'll take Walter out of here, and Helen too, and see if you can't get some real rest for a change. I'll bet that's all that's wrong with you.'

'No, I don't think that's all that's wrong. But, yes, I will try to sleep.'

Walter rose and smiled tenderly down upon her. 'And you used to think Liza didn't care about you. I suppose now you'll admit you were foolish.'

Jennifer felt a sinking sensation within her. 'Yes, I was foolish. About Liza, among other things.'

Without the pain, she had no difficulty falling asleep as soon as they were gone. She sank into an exhausted slumber, only to be awakened some time later by the sound of her bedroom door softly opening and closing.

She opened her eyes and saw Bess, and Mrs. Hodges, hobbling across the room toward her.

'My, my, it looks like you've had a sinking spell, dearie,' Mrs. Hodges greeted her.

'Mrs. Hodges, oh, thank you for coming.' Jennifer struggled to a sitting position in the bed. 'I was afraid you might refuse.'

'Always glad to be of help.' She leaned over the bed until Jennifer could again smell that foul breath. 'If I can be of help, that is.' she cocked an eyebrow.

Jennifer reached out and touched her hand. It was dry and coarse, like the bark of an old tree. 'She's killing me.'

Mrs. Hodges nodded head sagely. 'Yes, she is.'

'You must help me. I don't think I could survive another of those attacks. Tell me how to stop her.'

'I've already told you what to do.' Mrs. Hodges reached into her pocket and brought out the doll she had made to represent Liza. 'Here's the answer. I even brought you my pin. You stick that through the heart and your troubles will be over.'

At the door, Bess's eyes were like saucers.

'I can't,' Jennifer said with a groan. 'I can't resort to murdering her.'

'Well, that's up to you, I'm sure.' Mrs. Hodges drew herself up indignantly. 'You asked for my help. There it is. Use it or not, as you like.' She started for the door.

'Wait. Surely there must be something else you can do, something you can give me that would not harm her.'

Mrs. Hodges turned from the door. 'She's got the power,' she said in a voice of scorn, 'and she's got the doll. So long as she's alive, your life isn't worth that.' She snapped her fingers. 'Now, I'll be going, thank you. Call on me if you need anything. If you can call on me, that is.'

She went out with a final, withering look at Jennifer. Bess followed her to see her out of the house.

Jennifer looked at the doll Mrs. Hodges had left lying on the bed. She picked it up and repressed a shudder. What an innocent looking thing, to be so evil.

She heard someone coming along the hall and quickly thrust the doll and the pin under her pillow. A moment later Liza came into the room. She shut the door soundly after herself and leaned against it.

'I saw her,' she said in a low, menacing voice. Her eyes flashed wickedly and her entire face was contorted into a mask of rage and hatred.

'Saw who?'

'Mrs. Hodges.' Liza fairly spat the name out. 'So that's how you got Walter interested in you again, is it? I should have known it was some of her doing.'

Now, for the first time Jennifer saw Liza as she truly was, full-grown in malevolence.

'Walter never really went away from me. He loves me, you know. Nothing you can do will change that.'

An evil smile played upon Liza's lips. 'Oh, but you're wrong. There *is* something I can do. You thought that witch's potions would solve everything, did you? You don't learn your lessons very well for a schoolteacher. I will see to it there is nothing of you to love.'

'What do you mean?' Jennifer was truly alarmed now.

Liza laughed and it sounded to Jennifer exactly like the laugh of the old woman in the swamp. 'You know just what I mean. I had to kill Alicia to get her out of the way and I'll do the same to you.'

'You can't get away with it.' Jennifer sat up again, struggling to get out of her bed.

'Who's going to blame me? They already all think you're crazy, the same as Alicia. And Walter won't be in such a hurry to marry again. This time he'll wait, wait for me.'

'You're mad.' Jennifer had gotten her feet on the floor. With all the strength she could summon, she shoved herself away from the bed, lunging toward Liza, but Liza sidestepped and gave Jennifer a cruel shove. She fell to the floor.

'You'll never feel Walter's arms around you again,' Liza said. With that she was gone, disappearing from the room.

14

Downstairs, Helen and Bess heard Jennifer fall and hurried up to her room. They found her barely conscious on the floor, and between them they managed to get her onto her bed. As they did so, they moved her pillow, to reveal the doll lying there, a pin beside it.

Helen had grown up in New Orleans, where voodoo was an everyday matter, and she had lived much of her life in the bayous. She snatched up the doll, recognizing it at once for what it was.

Jennifer gasped in agony, feeling once again the familiar tightening at her throat, cutting off her breath. Would it get tighter and tighter this time until she could not breathe at all?

Helen looked at the doll in her hand, and at Jennifer, struggling for breath, and finally at Bess. Bess met her gaze frankly, and nodded her head.

'Yes,' she said. 'It's Liza. She's got a

doll of Miss Jennifer. And the swamp witch, she brought Jennifer this one, she said the only way to stop Liza is to stick a pin through that.'

'I can't do it,' Jennifer groaned.

'That girl is killing Jennifer,' Bess said. 'This time for sure.'

For a long moment Helen hesitated. She looked again at Jennifer, whose face had begun to turn blue.

'No,' Helen said. 'No, she is not.' With a swift, determined gesture she thrust the pin straight through the breast of the doll. The air was rent with a terrible scream. At once Jennifer could breathe again, the pressure was gone from her throat.

'I . . . I couldn't . . . ' she said.

'I'm older than you,' Helen said. 'I learned a long time ago, sometimes you have to fight evil on its own terms.'

'And Liza . . . ?'

Helen looked at the doll in her hand, the pin sticking out of it. 'She's dead,' Helen said.

Jennifer looked at the other two women. Neither of them showed any sign of remorse at what had just happened.

'But, what will we tell Walter?' Jennifer asked after a long silence. 'How can we explain . . . ?'

'We can't,' Helen said. 'He'd never understand, not in a million years.'

'But . . . '

'She ran away before, there's nothing to say she wouldn't again,' Helen said. 'Those swamps, those black waters, they could hide a thousand dark secrets. Walter and all the men are out in the fields. Even Peter and Mary are with them. There's no one to see Bess and me carry a bundle out of the house. Once she's been tossed into the water, she'll never be found. If you'll help me, Bess?' she added, giving Bess a questioning glance.

'Yes'm,' Bess said. 'I'll be mighty happy to have that evil out of the house.'

* * *

Helen and Bess had barely finished with their grisly chore when Bess came to Jennifer's bedroom to announce, 'There's someone here to see you.' She had an odd look, Jennifer thought. Frightened, but not only that.

'To see me?' Jennifer was expecting no one. Could someone have sent for Doctor Goodman? 'Is he in the parlor?'

'She came up here with me,' Bess said, seeming to grope for the right words. She was saved the necessity of further explanation. Before she could say more, the door was pushed open and Mrs. Hodges came into the room.

'In the parlor? Oh, my,' she said, laughing. 'It's only me, dearie. No need to be formal. You know, this is a pretty room, ain't it?'

Jennifer could feel the skin tingle on the back of her neck. 'What do you want?' she asked coldly.

'What do I want? Dearie, I've come to see you. Isn't that enough?'

'Do you want money?'

'Money? Why, you offered me that before, didn't you? Didn't need it then and don't need it now.' Mrs. Hodges looked around at Bess. 'You don't need to stay.'

'No, stay, Bess, do,' Jennifer said.

'I'll stay too,' Helen said, coming into the room. 'There's nothing you can say to Jennifer that we can't hear.'

'Seems to me like you were a lot happier to see me last time I come here.' Mrs. Hodges face took on a sly expression. 'Of course, the girl child was still here then, tormenting you.'

'What do you mean?' She and Bess and Helen exchanged glances.

'She's gone, now, ain't she?'

'What makes you say that?' Jennifer asked.

'She is gone, that's all. And I know how, too.'

'If you think that I . . . '

'Don't matter who. It's done, is the important thing. And seeing as you all seem to be so close together, I guess we all know what was done.'

Jennifer gave her an icy glare. 'Whatever you think you know, you have no proof of it. None anyone would believe. Now, if you want money, I will arrange for some to be sent to you. I have none on hand. But I forbid you to enter this house again. If you do, I shall have you whipped and sent away.'

Mrs. Hodges threw back her head and cackled with glee.

'Whipped,' she gasped, hardly able to speak. 'Whipped, she says. Oh, my, dearie, you are a riot, ain't you? She's going to have me whipped for coming into my own home.'

It was like a slap in the face. Jennifer's cheeks burned. At the same moment, Mrs. Hodges laughter stopped as suddenly as if it had been cut with a knife.

'What did you say?' Helen asked.

'I said, my home,' Mrs. Hodges said, her expression no longer even amused. 'My shack caught on fire. I don't have a home there now, and since we're all such good friends, helping one another out and all, I knew you'd want me to come here and consider this my home.'

'No,' Jennifer said. 'I will give you what jewelry I have. It will fetch a good price in New Orleans, and if you'll send me your address, I will see that you receive assistance regularly, but you must not come back here.'

She went to her dresser for her jewel

case and brought it back, but Mrs. Hodges just ignored it. Instead, she went to the little upholstered chair by the bed.

'My, this is comfortable,' she said. 'I hope you've got a room as nice as this for me. Oh, and thank you, but I couldn't go to New Orleans, dearie, I'm no good at traveling anymore. Besides, I've lived here all my life, I wouldn't know how to get along in the city. No, us birds of a feather got to stick together. That's what I always told Liza. Course, she wouldn't listen, thought she could just ditch me when she got what she wanted. But you saw where that got her. I told her, first time she asked for my help, I said, if you don't want to stew, don't get in the pot. But she wouldn't listen. No, we're friends now, all four of us, it seems. And don't anyone be forgetting, what I did for Liza, and for you, dearie, I could do again.'

'You're threatening me with another of your dolls?' Jennifer asked.

'Now, I wouldn't want to put it just like that. But things could happen, is what I'm saying.'

'Yes,' Bess said, stepping forward. She

put her hand in the pocket of her apron and brought out the witch's bottle her Auntie Doreen had given her. 'Just think what would happen if I was to plant this out in the yard.'

Mrs. Hodges eyes went wide. 'Where did you get that? Give that to me.' She reached to snatch the bottle from Bess' hand, but Bess was too quick for her. Mrs. Hodges glowered at her for a moment. ''Sides, it's got no power. You got nothing of mine in it.'

'Are you so sure? Last night, before your shack burned down — did you remember to empty your chamber pot?'

Mrs. Hodges looked frightened, her eyes going from one to the other of the women in the room. 'You're just trying to scare me.'

'Suit yourself,' Bess said. 'I'm going down now and bury this bottle. You can stick around and see what happens, if you want to. If I was you, though, I'd want to get as far away as I could, as quick as I could.'

There was a long moment of silence. 'If I go,' Mrs. Hodges said finally, 'you'll wait a while before you bury that?'

Helen looked at the clock on the mantle. 'We'll give you two hours.'

For another moment Mrs. Hodges glared angrily at the three of them. Then, muttering under her breath, she waddled toward the door. 'Just remember, there's powers and then there's powers.'

'No threats,' Helen said. 'If anyone in this household takes sick, we'll know just what to do.'

With one final, venomous glance, the swamp witch was gone.

★   ★   ★

Later, Walter discovered that Liza had vanished.

'Maybe she went back to the swamp,' Jennifer suggested innocently.

Walter went to see, and came back with the news that Mrs. Hodges' shack had burned to the ground, and there was no trace of her or Liza.

'They must have gone off somewhere together,' Helen said. 'She was a strange girl, Walter. I always looked for her to vanish again someday.'

For a bit, Walter looked gloomy and dispirited, and Jennifer wondered if he might still be under some kind of spell Liza had cast on him.

'Just so long as you don't go and disappear,' he told Jennifer, taking her in his arms.

'There's no magic strong enough to make me do that,' she said.

THE END

Other titles in the
Linford Mystery Library:

DEADLY MEMOIR

Ardath Mayhar

When Margaret Thackrey, ex-government agent and writer, decides to pen her memoirs, she unwittingly gets the attention of a vicious assassin — a man whose nefarious deeds she'd nearly uncovered during her service. Now he must stop the publication of her book before his true character is revealed. He murders Margaret's husband, and stalks her from Oregon to Texas, where she must finally confront her past — and a determined, stone-cold killer!

THE GRAB

Gordon Landsborough

In Istanbul, a beautiful girl is grabbed from her hotel bed and taken out into the night. But Professional Trouble-Buster Joe P. Heggy is looking on and decides to investigate: who was the girl and why was she kidnapped? But when thugs try to eliminate him, he is equal to their attempts, especially when he's aided by a bunch of American construction workers. Then things get very tense when Heggy finds the girl — and then kidnaps her himself . . .

THE PURPLE GLOVE MURDERS

Mary Wickizer Burgess

In Southern California, Gail Brevard and her law partner Conrad 'Connie' Osterlitz are relaxing at their mountain hideaway. When retired Justice Winston Craig is found dead, face down on Black Bear Lake, Gail is asked to find the cause of his death. She becomes convinced it is linked to one of his old cases. However, when Connie is attacked and lies near death, Gail must use all her resources to solve the crime before it's too late . . .

A HEART THAT LIES

Steve Hayes and Andrea Wilson

Jackie O'Hara has been in a race against time. Terminally ill, she's determined to make peace with her estranged brother, yet there is just one problem — first, she must find him. Meanwhile, Danny is being chased by the Russian Mafia who want him dead, and Interpol, who need him to testify against mob boss Dmitri Kaslov. That makes Jackie a target as well, because they all hope she will lead them straight to him . . .